# DATING & DRAGONS

---

IVY COLLINS

STARWATCH PRESS

1

———

## OLIVIA

*A* very pretty man in fake elf ears sweeps past me as I stand in line, and I can't help but think I don't belong here.

So many other people in this line are dressed up in costumes, or wearing shirts from previous convention years. There are whole families in proud TowerCon shirts —even a baby, in a *My First TowerCon* onesie. Any given person here could probably rattle off the rules to *Towers & Tyrants* by heart. Heck, I bet the *baby* knows more about those funny-looking dice they use to play the game than I do.

But my new roommate Emily *insisted* that I had to come with her to this convention, and I want to get along with her so badly. I'm just finishing the tail end of my degree in technical writing while working my butt off at a local coffee chain, and I still don't have many friends in

Dallas. Emily is gorgeous, outgoing, friendly—and absolutely obsessed with *Towers & Tyrants*. She says she wants to introduce me to her T&T group, but since they're all seventh-level characters already, I've got to play a few rounds as a newbie at this convention before I join them. *I figure a first-level game will be less intimidating for you to start,* Emily told me.

So here I am, surrounded by people ten times more thrilled to be here. It's not that I think this is beneath me —in fact, it's the exact opposite. I'm scared that I don't belong here—that I'm trying to fool everyone at this convention into believing I can be a part of their hobby. I know it involves math, and lots of different dice, and multiple rulebooks... and maybe the truth is that I think it's a little too *smart* for someone like me.

The line moves forward, and I hurry to move with it. Em is supposed to get off work by noon. I'm supposed to get my badge before she shows up. Judging from the speed of the line, I'll have a few hours to kill before she meets me... but I'm intimidated by the crowd, and I'm starting to think I might just slip away to grab a coffee until then.

"You look *terrified,*" a man behind me observes. I turn in place, frowning... and my mouth goes dry.

He's a full head taller than I am, with messy black hair and warm brown eyes. He's wearing a short-sleeved shirt that clings to his hard, muscled frame, with the words *Gaming for Puppies* printed across the front. I find myself wondering whether someone had to pour him into those tight, acid-washed jeans that cling to his long legs.

"Are you okay?" he asks me. There's something about

his voice that makes my legs extra weak, even as I note the sincerity in his tone. He's got a low baritone made for murmuring—the kind of voice that sinks into your bones and makes you vibrate pleasantly.

*Don't think about vibrating!* I think to myself, mortified. *That is absolutely the last thing you should be thinking of right now. Whatever you do, do NOT talk about things that vibrate.*

I open my mouth… but all that comes out is a choked little noise.

The friendly guy behind me frowns and reaches into his side bag, pulling out a fresh bottle of water and pushing it into my hands. "Here," he offers. "Take this. Do you need to sit down somewhere? This crowd can be a bit much."

I take the bottled water dumbly. His warm fingers brush across mine, and I feel a jolt right down to my core. Good god, I'm hopelessly attracted to this man. And worse—he seems *nice*.

"Next!" calls a voice behind me. I glance that way wildly and see that an attendant has split the line. I'm supposed to go up to one of the counters to buy my badge.

"Hey, good timing," says the guy that's just melted my insides. "Come on, let's get you sorted." He smiles encouragingly at me and offers me a hand. "I'm Finn, by the way. I'm kind of a volunteer here."

I stare at his hand for an extra long second, before my brain catches up and tells me I'm supposed to take it. I curl my fingers around his, and the stress of the crowd *does* ease somewhat.

"I'm… Olivia," I manage finally, in a hoarse voice that

makes me wince. "Nice to meet you, Finn. I'm sorry I'm such a mess. I *really* don't know what I'm doing here."

Finn smiles at me again and tugs me gently toward the counter. "So you're a first-timer!" he says. "Even better. I love introducing people to the con."

The volunteer behind the counter—*Dave,* according to his name tag—looks up at us as we approach. He's probably a year or two younger than I am, but he hasn't quite filled out yet, so he *feels* like a kid to me in comparison. Dave's face brightens as he sees Finn. "Hey dude!" he says. "Always good to see you." Dave settles his eyes on me next, and he grins. "Did you bring your girlfriend this year?"

My face heats up instantly, and Finn coughs on a laugh. "I just met her two seconds ago," he tells Dave. "She's new to the con—I just wanted to make sure she didn't get trampled." Finn glances down at me with a rueful grin, and I instantly forgive any awkwardness from the exchange. "Did you need a badge, Olivia?" he asks.

I press my lips together. "Um, yeah," I say slowly. "I'm pretty sure this is where I get one?"

"You'd be right," Dave tells me cheerfully. "Did you want a pass just for today, or did you want a weekend pass?"

My mind blanks. I don't know the answer to that question. I know I'm supposed to find a beginner's game to play with Em, but I don't know when those actually happen. "Um," I say again, embarrassed. "I really don't know. There's *Towers & Tyrants* games here, right?" Duh. I try not to smack myself in the face at the obviousness. *TowerCon.* "I mean *beginner's* games," I add hastily, hoping I haven't just revealed my stupidity. "Like first-level games. Is there one of those this weekend? Which day would that be?"

Dave grins past my shoulder. I realize he's sharing a look with Finn, behind me.

"Why yes," Finn says, with humor in his voice. "We *do* have one of those." He reaches past me and sets down a bill. "Get her a weekend badge, Dave? And I think you've got my badge behind the counter somewhere too, if you don't mind."

I crane my head to look back at Finn, blinking. "Oh!" I say. "Oh man, you don't have to do that—"

Finn dazzles me with another of those heart-melting smiles. "I know I don't *have* to," he says. "Just think of it as encouragement to come back next year."

Dave rummages behind the counter and pulls out a blank badge for me. He hands me a sharpie to write my name on it. As I do, I catch sight of the pre-printed badge he hands to the man behind me. It's a more official-looking badge than mine, with a different color around the border to make it stand out. *Finn O'Roarke*, it says in big text. Then, in smaller text beneath, it says: *Celebrity Gamemaster*.

I frown to myself. I know, in very loose terms, that a gamemaster runs *T&T* games. I may not understand all of the details involved in that part, but I do know what the word *celebrity* means.

"I'm running a first-level game in about fifteen minutes," Finn tells me. "It's technically full, but I think we can slip an extra player in at the table, if you want to join us."

I catch a whiff of his warm, earthy scent as he slides past me; a few of the excited people in line are less than squeaky clean, given the Texas heat, but if there's any sweat on Finn, it's the kind that makes me want to lick his skin.

*Stop that!* I think hysterically. *No vibrating and no skin-licking, for god's sake. You're going to scare this very nice, very hot man away from you in no time.*

Finn picks up my hand in his, blissfully unaware of my thoughts as he helps me through the crowd. "Do you have any idea of the sort of character you'd like to play?" he asks me conversationally, as we wind our way out of the press of people.

"I have no idea," I confess to him. "My roommate lent me her books, but I didn't really know where to start. I think... is there some kind of knight I could play? Can women be knights in this game?"

Finn smiles at that, as though I've just said something adorable. His brown eyes sparkle. "Anyone can be *anything* in this game," he assures me. "And yeah—I think we can make you a knight. How do you feel about crusaders?"

A silly grin splits across my face. It's partially the company—it would be stupid to pretend I don't like having this gorgeous man's attention all to myself, even for just a few minutes. But part of it is the ease with which he says I can be a knight.

I always wanted to swing a sword at someone.

"I like where your head is at," I tell him.


**FINN**

The adorable girl-next-door I found in line is named Olivia—and when I tell her she can play a knight, she lights up like I've just promised to make her a movie star.

It's a good thing I've got experience writing gaming books on the side. I only have about ten more minutes to explain the basics about Olivia's starter character to her. It's one I always have on hand—I wrote it myself, when I was putting together the lore for my favorite god from the official setting. *First-Level Paladin of Luin* is the generic name at the top of the sheet. The tenets of the god of beauty are listed in a small sidebar on the print-out. I explain to Olivia that this is the code of conduct by which her character behaves.

"*A wicked heart can never be beautiful,*" Olivia reads out loud, as she pushes back a few loose strands of her mousy brown hair. She purses her lips in surprise. "I like that. It's poetic."

I try not to look too flattered. I wrote all the tenets myself, after all. Almost anyone else at TowerCon would know that; but Olivia hasn't even cracked a sourcebook, let alone any of the side supplements. "Luin is the god of art and beauty," I tell her. "He was born very beautiful himself, but at some point in the lore, he was horribly scarred across his face. It made him change his idea of what beauty was, or ought to be."

"*Imperfections are human, and therefore worthy of love,*" Olivia reads out, as she continues down the list. She smiles at that. "Ah, I think I'm starting to get the gist. I like him. So, I'm playing one of Luin's knightly servants?"

"That's right," I tell her. "You're mostly a fighter type, but you've got a handful of holy powers. As you get higher level, you'll get more of those—but you'll probably only hit level two by the end of this game."

Olivia was horrifically nervous when I first found her

in line—but now that she's holding this sheet in her hands, she just looks utterly thrilled. Her hazel eyes sparkle with that special excitement I only get to see in brand new players. I have to hold myself back from overwhelming her with all my favorite bits of lore. There's so much written *and* unwritten setting development at this point that that kind of conversation could take days. Besides, I find myself a little curious to see how a brand new player might interpret this character, without a whole chapter's worth of background to prepare her.

"Do I just use my normal name?" Olivia asks me, as she looks down at the words *First-Level Paladin of Luin*. "Am I like... Sir Liv?"

I chuckle at that. "No, no... I mean, not unless you really want to be called Sir Liv. A few people do use their real name, when they can't come up with a different one in the moment."

Olivia stares down at the sheet, scrunching up her nose thoughtfully, and I get the strangest impulse to lean down and kiss the very tip of it.

*Woah,* I think. *That was... odd.* I shake myself a bit and blink. I'm probably just running on too little sleep. My badge might say *Celebrity Gamemaster*, but gamewriting doesn't pay the bills quite as well as my day job. I've been going to work nine to five during the week and staying up late prepping for the convention for a few nights in a row now.

"How about *Elsinore?*" Olivia says. She looks up at me, clearly trying to gauge my approval. As though I'm going to tell her certain names are against the rules.

"Dame Elsinore?" I suggest.

Olivia brightens at that, and starts searching around

for something to write with. I guide her over toward the gaming table where we're supposed to begin and snatch her up a pencil from the center.

"Hey guys," I address the players already gathered there. "Sorry for cutting it close. I found a stray and decided to bring her home." A few of the players chuckle obligingly on cue. "This is Olivia. It's her first time at the convention, and her very first T&T game. I hope you all don't mind if she joins us. I wanted to make sure she had a fantastic first time."

*Er.* That came out a little awkward, now that I replay the words in my head. But everyone at the table knows what I mean, and no one seems to have gone looking for any innuendo. Olivia blushes, but that's probably just because she's suddenly the center of attention.

"Totally for it!" one of the guys at the table assures us both. "What are you playing, Olivia?"

I grab her a chair, since we're one short. Olivia settles into it with a bewildered smile at me, looking at the friendly faces around her. "I'm a paladin of Luin," she says. "None of you have wicked hearts, do you?"

One of the guys across from her—a blond in a nice black button-down—has to stifle a snicker. "Oh boy," he says. "I'm playing a lawful evil character. I'll try to keep it low-key, don't worry."

Olivia raises an eyebrow at him. She glances down at the tenets on her sheet. "*Wicked hearts may change, when offered beautiful words and beautiful actions,*" she tells him stubbornly.

I feel a sudden surge of irrational pride at that. "I think she's catching on," I observe. "This should be an interesting game, everyone."

2

## OLIVIA



**TWO YEARS AGO.**

*I* love this game.

Well, maybe it's more appropriate to say: I love this character. I love this *gamemaster*. Finn is the one driving the story along. He sets every scene for us, painting atmosphere and little details and acting out the non-player characters we meet along the way. Every time we meet someone new, he changes his voice and affects a totally different attitude. At one point, he's an old crone we meet along the road, who turns out to be a faerie in disguise. Later, he's an arrogant priest of Urdal, the god of gold and mercenaries.

The game is far more intricate than I'd been led to believe. We're not just killing goblins; our party finds itself asked to take sides in a dispute between the local faeries that live in the woods and the nearby town that's been cutting down their trees. I end up in an involved discussion with Luke, the player who warned me he was playing a lawful evil character. He makes a number of greedy, self-serving points, which I counter with my god's tenets. We're both having fun with it, and I can tell that Finn is enjoying it too, by the way he leans back in his chair and grins at us.

"I really don't care which side we take, as long as *someone* pays us," Luke sighs at me in his character's voice. "Tell me, Elsinore, does your god find *money* beautiful?"

I narrow my eyes at him. "Some day," I tell him, "I hope that you learn to find comfort in something other than gold. But for now, since money is what you hold so dear—*I* will pay you, so that you might do the right thing."

Luke blinks, and shifts out of character. "Really?" he says. "I mean... it's a cool idea, but I don't know if it's soci-ety-legal."

I frown, puzzled. "Society-legal?" I ask.

"We're playing an official Tower Society game right now," one of the other guys tells me. There's a little note-card sitting in front of him that reminds me his actual name is *Bart*. "They've got standard adventures and approved gamemasters. At the end of the session, you'll get to keep your character and an equal share of the trea-sure we all earn here, and you can keep playing Elsinore in other society games."

Luke shoots me a wry smile. "I like your thinking," he tells me, "but I'm not sure Tower Society would let me take your part of the gold. Honestly, I wouldn't feel great taking it from you out-of-character, either. I'm not *really* a greedy son of a bitch."

Finn leans in over the table. "I think we can work out a compromise, if everyone's amenable," he says. "Luke, we'll let the scene continue as it's already been going. Why don't we let Liv roll Elsinore's diplomacy? If she makes the roll, maybe your character has a moment of doubt and gives her back her gold by the end of the game?"

Luke lights up. "I like that too!" he says. I reach for the dice, but he holds up a hand. "Nah, don't even roll. I'm gonna fail on purpose. I may not shift his alignment permanently or anything, but it'll make for a good role-playing moment."

I can't help but smile at that. "Aw, thanks," I say, embarrassed. "I didn't mean to cause some kind of trouble with the rules, but I like that solution."

Finn looks like he's impressed with both of us, even though I've just thrown the whole game for a loop. "It's not a problem at all," he assures me. "This is exactly the kind of stuff I love seeing at the table. For someone who just picked up a character an hour ago, you're doing a fantastic job."

My cheeks heat up, and I have to work not to wriggle down in my seat.

We do end up in a few fights. I learn to roll a d20—a twenty-sided die—to see if I hit with my sword, and a d8 to determine my damage. But by the end of the game, we actually manage to work out a peace agreement between the two sides, and I get to make a diplomacy check to encourage them both to accept it.

A whole table full of strangers takes the time to tell me what a delight it was to play with me. Luke shakes my hand and promises to think on his wicked heart. I find myself sitting with my character sheet, beaming like an idiot.

*This isn't so hard,* I think. *I've even got a character now!*

I wonder if Emily's T&T group is society-legal. Would they let me bring in Elsinore? Wait, Emily said they're higher level—

"Hey," Finn says next to me. His voice feels closer than it really is, the way it sends butterflies fluttering inside my stomach. "I've got to grab lunch before my next game. You want to join me?"

I glance up at him, and my body heats up. He's got such a sincere smile on his face as he looks down at me. He's leaning in just close enough that I can feel his warmth.

"Lunch sounds great," I say, before I can stop myself.


## FINN

I love this woman.

I mean, I love the way she plays her *character.* That's what I mean to say.

Olivia really jumps right into things, determined to puzzle out how to play her background. She clearly isn't any sort of polished actor, but she's already memorized her god's tenets—and lord, she ends up in an actual *philosophical argument* at the table, with the other players jumping in to take sides. It's the first time I've ever seen a player embrace my favorite creation with such genuine enthusiasm.

I'm glad that Olivia lingers a bit longer than the others. I want to take her to lunch and pick her brain, to hear how she enjoyed her first game ever. She smiles up at me—and again, I get that funny urge to lean down and brush my lips over hers, just to see how they taste.

*You don't even know if she's dating someone,* I think suddenly. *Calm down. The last thing you want to do is harass some new player at your table just because she's cute.*

"Lunch sounds great," Olivia tells me, before I can get too caught up in the thought.

I pull out her chair and help her up, and she walks beside me as I head for the sandwich place just around the corner from the convention hall. "Do you think paladins of Luin often redeem people?" Olivia asks me as we walk. Her mind is already spinning up interesting scenarios, as fast as I can answer her questions. "I imagine they'd have to spend a lot of time hanging out with the same person to really get them to rethink their life choices."

"It's one of Luin's main tenets," I tell her, bemused. "So I imagine some paladins really do put in that kind of work. Some less savory people figure they can take advantage of Luin's people because of that. But I like to think his paladins really do make the people around them better in the long run."

Olivia nods seriously. She's taking in all of this bit by bit, stashing it away in the back of her head for some purpose I don't yet understand. "I think I want Elsinore to have the chance to redeem someone," she tells me. "Especially someone who really doesn't *want* to be redeemed. That sounds like a lot of fun. But I'm not sure that kind of plot would work out if I'm jumping between these one-time society games, would it?"

"No," I say slowly. "I don't think a bunch of society one-shots would be a good fit for a plot arc like that." A thought slowly rises to the top of my mind. "Do you live here in Dallas, Olivia?"

Olivia shoots me a surprised look. "Oh, yeah," she says. "I mean, not *in* Dallas, but close enough. Why?"

I mentally apologize to Future Me. He's about to have a lot of new work on his plate. "I'm local too," I tell her. "I'm about to finish up the game I've been running for the last few years. If you want, I can add you to the new game I'm working on, once this one is over. You could play Elsinore, and we could talk about your plot idea."

Olivia's eyes widen. "Really?" she says. I can tell this lunch is about to get a lot more interesting. "Oh, wow. That's... that's really nice of you. I would *love* that."

*Sorry, Future Me,* I think. *The cute girl with the paladin makes a great argument.*

I spend a little bit more time filling Olivia in on the lore behind her god. She's now so over the moon that she's settled in right next to me in the booth and pulled a notebook from her bag to start taking notes. I'm having problems with her sitting so close to me. Olivia radiates warmth like a heater—it's summer in Texas, and I don't even care. I can see every little freckle on her nose, and every thoughtful twist of her pink-tinted lips. Her hair smells like some kind of sharp apple shampoo, and I *know* I absolutely shouldn't be noticing that as much as I do.

I'm not just attracted to her. I'm in... *adorable* with her. Is that a thing? I just can't get over how sweet and charming she is. It makes me want to wrap her up in my arms and kiss every one of those freckles on her face. It's an incredibly conflicted feeling, because I'm *also* itching to get my hands all over her naked skin, and *none* of these things are in any way appropriate.

We're partway through eating our sandwiches when Olivia's cell phone rings, breaking me out of these thoughts. She blinks down at it.

"Oh!" Olivia manages. "Sorry, I have to take this! One second." She answers the phone. "Hey, Em. Yeah, I got my badge. I already played a game! The gamemaster was great—we're at lunch now." Olivia carefully doesn't meet my eyes as she says this, and I find my lips twitching.

The person on the other end keeps talking. Olivia mentions the sandwich place we're at, then sneaks another peak at my badge. "Finn O'Roarke?" she tells the person on the other end of the line. She shoots me an apologetic glance. "Is that how you say your last name? I should have asked."

The phone goes silent for a second.

The door to the restaurant opens, and I see a tall, redheaded woman in low-heeled boots burst inside. She's half dressed-up for the con, in colored contacts and a dress with an impressive hand-stitched symbol of Egala, goddess of birds. It's an incredibly professional-looking cosplay of an iconic character from the core T&T book, so I suspect she's got a proper wig and the rest of the costume still sitting in a car somewhere. She searches the booths until she finds the two of us, and her mouth drops.

"How on earth did you get a ticket to one of O'Roarke's games?" Olivia's friend asks with an incredulous laugh. She shakes her head at me. "I thought they booked all your table slots months ago!"

Olivia blinks, and I do my best not to look embarrassed. "Olivia looked a little lost," I say diplomatically. "When I found out she'd never played before, everyone was nice enough to make her a bit of room."

Olivia's redheaded friend extends her hand to me, and I reach out to shake it. "I'm Emily," she introduces herself. "I *loved* your *Divine Compendium*. I tore my first one up so bad, I had to get a leather-bound copy."

I nod sagely. "Clearly," I tell her, "you're a woman of class, Emily. As evidenced by your fantastic taste in authors."

Olivia glances over at me. "Oh!" she says. "No wonder you know so much about all these gods. You wrote a book on them?"

"He wrote *the* book on them," Emily tells Olivia wryly. "Or... the supplement, anyway." I'm suddenly embarrassingly glad to have a fan nearby to extol my virtues. Emily is already doing a fantastic job, if the dawning realization on Olivia's face is anything to go by.

"Oh my god," Olivia says. "I am so sorry. I bet all those people at your table spent extra money to be there, didn't they?"

I shake my head quickly. "No, they didn't," I assure her. "They just entered a lottery. Once they got in, they paid the same amount for the event as they would for any other table."

Olivia continues speaking, with dawning panic on her face. "And here I've been talking your ear off about stuff for my character that probably doesn't fit at *all* with the stuff you've already written—"

"It's just fine!" I assure her quickly. "It's fantastic, actually. I'm really looking forward to it."

Emily knits her brow at me. "Looking forward to..."

She turns her attention toward Olivia, who shrinks a little into the booth.

"I'm gonna be in Finn's group, for his next local game," Olivia mumbles.

Emily closes her eyes and presses her fingers to her forehead. "...I am very happy for you, Liv," she says slowly, as though she's trying to convince herself that this is, indeed, the case. "I was really hoping you'd enjoy the con. And it sounds like you really have."

Olivia's sheepish expression is about to cause further problems for Future Me.

"Would you like to join the game too, Emily?" I ask politely. "I haven't finalized the group yet."

Emily raises her eyebrows at me. Slowly, she slides into the booth next to her friend.

"Okay," she says to Olivia. "I admit, I owe you one. I'm doing the dishes for the next two weeks."

3

OLIVIA



"Roland looks down at you with a cold laugh." Finn narrates the scene in a low tone, his voice laden with tension. "*Is this the best that a paladin of Luin has to offer? he sneers. I suppose I should expect no better from the god of beauty. In the end, you really are nothing but a pretty face, Dame Elsinore.*"

I groan and cover my face. I'm supposed to be the group's tank—but here I am with only four hit points left, with the big bad talking down to me. It's a real testament to Finn's ability as a gamemaster that we all so desperately want to punch him in the face.

"I want to kill him," I mutter. "I want to kill him *so bad* right now."

"Ugh, no kidding," Emily grumbles. "If you could only get over to me and heal me up to conscious, I could fry his ass. I've still got a fireball, Liv, I've been saving it *just* for him." If we were playing by stereotype, Emily really *should* have been the one playing a paladin of the god of beauty, instead of me. She's what most people envision when you say the word *bombshell*—just curvy enough, with hip-hugging slacks, low-heeled boots, and long red hair. But Emily isn't playing a paladin: she's playing a half-elven fashionista wizard named Julianna, and her character is currently bleeding out fifteen feet away from mine, at negative hit points.

"I'm *out* of healing, Em," I sigh, tearing my fingers through my hair in frustration. "Otherwise I wouldn't be standing here at four hit points, letting this asshole insult my god."

Finn leans back in his chair and grins, openly enjoying our angst. We're playing at his house in the suburbs, all settled around the living room coffee table. As is classic for Finn, he's over-prepared in every possible way: there's epic background music piping through his phone's speakers, and a custom-printed map of the encounter location. He's even 3D printed a figurine for the bad guy we've taken to calling Roland the Insufferable.

We've already spent two hours locked in glorious, round-by-round combat with Roland and his stupid pet clerics. I've used every ace I had up my sleeve—every item, every class ability. I know we've knocked the shit out of this guy—but we're all running on fumes, and Roland has had all his little minions healing him up every damned turn.

It's amazing. Even frustrated as I am, I can't help but be wildly impressed. Finn might be a sysadmin from nine to five, but *this* is where he belongs—sitting behind a gamemaster's screen, enjoying the lamentations of his players while he secretly roots for our last-minute dramatic success.

Finn's brown eyes sparkle at me with humor as I agonize, and I find myself torn between weirdly conflicted impulses. I want to strangle him, just a little bit. I also want to walk over to that office chair he's pulled over, straddle his lap, and kiss him until he can't breathe—

"Liv?" Samson snaps his fingers in front of my face, and I realize I've been staring at Finn for just a little bit too long. "Don't strangle our GM, sweetheart, we need him to finish the game. Let's strategize a little bit, huh? I'm down to cantrips, but I can still give you a plus one bonus to hit each round. What's that put you at?" Samson, playing our cleric of luck, Llew, is six feet and change of pure muscle—but he's always been the biggest teddy bear at the gaming table. Him and his husband Jim are playing married characters in-game, which is, *trust me,* just the most adorable thing in the world.

Samson has caught me out staring at our gamemaster though, and I blush furiously, ducking my head to glance at my character sheet. I've had to write out a set of temporary bonuses at the top just for this fight, due to all the buffs and debuffs flying around. "Um... okay," I manage. "That'll put me back at plus ten. That's not bad at all. We know Roland's not doing so hot himself, now that all his clerics are dead. I just have to last long enough to hit him a few times."

Samson nods seriously and nudges his husband. Jim, blond-haired and sweatervest-clad, adjusts his glasses at his own character sheet. "I'm out of inspiration for the day," Jim mutters, "but I can still go flank him and get you another bonus."

"Oh man," Emily snickers. "I'm just imagining our little bard, swiping at Roland with his lute." She leans over to mime herself smashing an instrument over Finn's head, and he plays along by cringing back, flinging his arms in front of his face.

"I am a *professional*, thank you very much," Jim huffs. He shoots me a smile. "I would never flank with a lute. That's what brass instruments are for."

I burst out laughing. "So... you've got a tuba on you, is what you're saying?"

That's the last straw. Soon we've all devolved into laughter, unable to progress. It takes another full minute before I catch my breath enough to reconsider the situation. "Okay," I manage. "I *know* I can hit Roland if you flank him, Jim. But I've still got to stay upright. So..." I eye Finn suspiciously, and that evil grin of his widens. "Take your best shot, Roland. I can do this all day."

Finn shakes his head and picks up his d20. "All right, let's do this," he says. "I'm rolling out in the open, so you can all see it. Your armor class hasn't changed, Liv, so he still needs a sixteen to hit you."

We're all leaning in as Finn rolls the die across the table. It clitter-clacks just past my own figurine, in a slow, dramatic tumble...

And comes up on eighteen.

We all groan at once. Even Finn looks a little bit abashed, as though he was hoping for a different number. "Oh, well," he sighs. "Let's roll damage..."

"I'm gonna die," I mutter. "Ugh, I'm so sorry, guys. Maybe Jim can still get in a lucky hit."

Jim plays a sad little trombone noise from his phone.

"Five damage," Finn tells me. He's smiling oddly though, and I knit my brow at him. That's his *I've-got-something-up-my-sleeve* smile.

"Well," I sigh. "I'm down for the count." But I keep my eyes on Finn, wondering what he's up to. His long fingers are drumming on the table next to him with anticipation.

"Uh... I guess I step up to attack him," Samson says. "I could always get a natural twenty—"

"Well, you're going to have to wait your turn," Finn interrupts. His grin is wide enough to split his face now. "There's someone else in the initiative order before you."

"There is?" Samson puzzles.

Emily gasps. "Oh man," she says. "Oh *man*. Please tell me it's who I think it is." She's bouncing up and down on the couch with glee now.

Finn flushes and manages an embarrassed laugh. "Um," he says. "Yes. A tall, wiry figure melts out of the shadows just next to your paladin. His shadowform breaks, as he pulls out a healing potion—"

Emily squeals. She looks like she's about to faint out of sheer, blissful fulfillment. I cover my mouth in shock. We only know one character who uses shadowform. His name is Keller, and he's a no-good scoundrel—better known by his moniker, the Prince of Thieves.

Or at least... Keller *was* a no-good scoundrel. Nearly since the beginning of the game, I've been working my butt off trying to convince him to be a better person. It's been kind of like dragging someone kicking and screaming into the light, but the whole thing has been a *terrible* lot of fun.

For the last year, Emily has been convinced that

Keller is in love with my paladin. It's her not-so-secret goal for the game to see me paired off with him. I've done my best not to encourage her too much, for... obvious reasons. Or maybe those reasons are only obvious to me.

Some players are better than others at separating in-game relationships from reality. As I stare at Finn's wry smile, my heart speeds up painfully. I'm already halfway in love with him in *real* life. I don't know if I can handle pretending to be in love with some tiny figment of his imagination.

"—and you regain fourteen hit points, Liv," Finn tells me, somehow managing a straight face. "You've only blacked out for a moment. But when you come back to consciousness, you see Keller leaning over you. *Don't you start, Sparrow,* he says. *I don't want to hear it.*"

*Sparrow.* My heart melts stupidly. It's a nickname Keller calls me. I mean... Elsinore. It's what he calls *Elsinore.*

"I can now die a happy woman," Emily declares. "I don't even need to roll my death save. I'll just bleed out over here on the ground and go to heaven satisfied."

"You little holy minx," Samson snorts at me. "I guess that last diplomacy check *did* do something, after all. You've charmed the Prince of Thieves into doing something useful for once in his life."

My face must be beet red by now. "Oh," I manage. It's not the witty rejoinder I wish I had. But am I crazy, or is there suddenly a strange heat between me and Finn? He's wearing that triumphant expression he normally has when he pulls off a plot reveal he's been waiting on for months. But there's a softness there too, and I can *feel* him waiting expectantly for my reaction.

The whole table is waiting for my reaction, actually. Jim has an eyebrow quirked in my direction. Samson has his character sheet in his hand, signalling that he's ready for his turn as soon as I get around to my reply. Emily is all but dying of anticipation.

*"You're late, Your Highness,"* I say finally, in the accent I use for my paladin. *"But I'll accept your apologies over dinner tonight."*

Emily sighs happily. Jim passes her the bowl of popcorn without a word, and she takes a handful as she watches me and Finn.

"I use my blessing of fortune on Elsinore," Samson says promptly. "Jim?"

"I get into flanking position with my mighty tuba," Jim replies, with a dry wit in his tone. "That's the end of the round, which makes it Liv's turn."

I grab my d20 and straighten in my seat, staring Finn in the eyes. "I get up and face down Roland," I declare. *"Luin is indeed the god of beauty. But his first tenet has always been thus: a wicked heart can never be beautiful."*

I roll the die in front of me. It skitters a few times, before coming to a dramatic stop... on a natural twenty.

"Yes!" Samson whoops. "Praise Luin, that's a critical! Roll that extra damage, Liv!"

"Uh oh," I say mildly. "I'm going to need another d8. Em, would you do the honors, please?"

Emily snatches up her sparkly blue d8 and shoves it into my hand. I roll the dice again and shoot a narrow smile at Finn. "That's fifteen damage," I tell him. "How does Roland the Insufferable feel about *that?*"

Finn sighs heavily. "Well," he says. "Being that he's

now very *dead*, I don't think Roland feels much of anything about it."

Samson hisses out a *yes!* Jim fumbles for his phone; the victory theme from his favorite video game cuts loudly across the table. Emily gets up to do a (somewhat salacious) touchdown dance.

I find myself smiling like a moron, riding the high. I'm a tank—not a hitter or a blaster—so it's rare that I get the final knock-out blow. But tonight, I got to beat our final boss by a hair, *and* my attempt at diplomacy last session actually paid off.

None of that is why I'm really melting on the inside, of course. I've committed every moment of that short interaction with Finn indelibly upon my memory. I'm sure I'll be replaying that wry smile and those brief, flirtatious words over and over in my mind for the next few weeks. *Sparrow.* I love the way he looks at me when he uses that nickname. No one's ever given me a nickname before.

*That's all in character,* I tell myself again, staring down at my character sheet. *Finn's just being a good storyteller. He's giving me the plot I said I wanted from the very beginning.*

"I figure that's a good place to pause for the night," Finn admits, once everyone settles down a bit. "I didn't intend to go quite so late—I've got to get to TowerCon bright and early tomorrow for setup."

I glance up at him, blinking. "Oh," I say. "Did you want some help? I'm scheduled to play in one of the early games anyway."

Finn gives me a wary look. "I'm organizing," he warns

me. "So I've got to be there *really* early. I'm sure you don't want to be in the car at six in the morning."

I snort. "I work in a coffee shop, Finn," I tell him. "I have to be up at *four* sometimes. I can be here by six, with java for both of us."

That wary look on Finn's face hesitates, and my heart jumps in my chest. He *wants* to say yes—I can see it in his eyes. Finn might not think packing game stuff at the crack of dawn sounds very exciting, but I'd get up far earlier in the morning for the chance at a little alone time with him. Just a few hours of his undivided attention, listening to him talk about his plans for the convention, shooting story ideas back and forth with him—

Emily coughs and leans forward to poke me in the stomach. I shoot her a furious look, and she jerks back, startled. "We have a thing, Liv," Emily mutters. "I mean... the *thing*, on Sunday. I just want to make sure you don't forget to bring your stuff tomorrow."

I have to take an extra second to remember what she's talking about. My eyes widen when I do. "Oh," I manage. "Yeah, don't worry—I'll pack that stuff you wanted."

Samson and Jim look away innocently from our exchange, trying not to let on that they know what's going on. Finn seems to realize something has flown over his head, but there's no way he could know what we're talking about. He clears his throat. "You really don't have to help out, if it's any trouble," he tells me.

I shake my head. "It's cool," I say. "It won't be a problem." I find myself biting at my lip as I look back over at him. "I *want* to."

That heat ratchets up between us again. I'm *sure* I'm not imagining it this time. His deep brown eyes meet mine, and I don't think either of us wants to look away. "Okay," Finn says softly. "Yeah. I'd like that."

* * *

"*Please* tell me you're going to ask him out," Emily begs me, as we settle into the car to head back to our apartment.

I drop my face into my hands. "Oh god," I say. "Please stop."

"I will *not!*" Emily declares. "Tonight was the most adorable, romantic thing I've ever seen. You have got to steal that yummy thief before someone else does, Liv."

I shoot her an incredulous glance between my fingers. "Are we talking about Finn right now, or Keller?"

"They're the same person, Liv!" Emily says in exasperation. She nudges me in the side with her elbow. "Oh, come on. Finn so clearly *adores* you. He's had a crush on you basically since this game started. Are you seriously telling me you haven't thought about it?"

My face is burning now. There's no point in denying it, so I don't. "He's just running a game, Em," I tell her. "Heck, your character ended up in a relationship with that barbarian, but that doesn't mean Finn wants to date *you.*"

"Of course not," Emily sniffs. "Finn's not my type, anyway. But I told him I wanted my dorky wizard to have a muscle man to ogle, and he obliged. It was very classy." She eyes me with a speculative expression. "Besides, tomorrow is the perfect opportunity. You'll have the whole morning with him to get your nerve up. And babe —your Sunday costume is *on-point.* That man would have to be made of stone to ignore you once you're all dressed up."

"Shh!" I hiss at her, glancing out the window toward Finn's house. He's still inside, and I relax. "We've spent like six months working on this, Em. I swear, if you wreck this surprise at the last second—"

"I would never!" Emily objects. "I made sure Finn wasn't out here. I could scream it out the window that you want to bone him, and he *still* wouldn't hear it. Here, let me show you."

Emily rolls down her car window and pushes herself outside before I can stop her. *"Finn and Livie, sittin' in a tree—"*

I scramble to haul her back from the window. "Oh god, oh god, *please* stop," I beg. My voice squeaks in horror. "I'm driving now, Em. Get your head inside."

Emily smirks at me as she settles back into her seat. "I bet you twenty bucks," she says. "Finn is going to kiss you before the end of the weekend."

I don't respond. But it's not because I think she's right.

I just want to dream that she is, for at least a little bit longer.

4

## FINN

Olivia shows up bright and early on my front porch, with two fresh coffees in hand. There's a queasy little hiccup in my chest as I see her outside, with the dawn light painted over her heart-shaped face. She's dressed a little more painstakingly than I normally see her, with a hint of tasteful makeup and the straps of a bright red, lacy summer bra-thing peeking out at the edges of her loose-knit shirt. (Is it a bra-lette? A mini-bra? Whatever they call those things, I suddenly thank the fashion gods that they've become popular.)

I get to spend the whole morning with Liv. Alone. Wearing that sexy lacy bra thing. I don't know what I did to deserve this unexpected blessing, but I need to figure out what it was so I can repeat it.

Olivia nudges the doorbell again with a puzzled look on her face, and I realize I've been staring through the window at her for the last few seconds, like a moron. I open the door hurriedly, and she beams as she sees me.

"Morning!" Liv chirps. "I got you a triple-shot, just for a bit of extra kick." She holds a steaming hot coffee cup out to me, and this is officially the best pre-convention morning I've *ever* had. I take it from her with a slow, tired blink.

"Wow," I manage. "You're looking..." Gorgeous. Tempting. *Still* adorable, somehow. I force my tired mind to search for an adjective that isn't going to get me in huge trouble here. "...alive," I finish finally. "No one should be this happy in the morning, Liv."

Olivia grins at me as she steps inside, and the corners of her eyes crinkle upward. "I *told* you I normally get up way earlier than this," she reminds me. "And this is way better than dragging my butt to work to make soy lattes for the yoga ladies."

I get a sudden image of Liv in yoga pants, and it does nothing to encourage my good behavior. I shake my head sharply, trying to dispel it. "Well... thanks for coming by to help," I tell her. "I really appreciate it."

I've got most of my game day stuff already prepared, sorted, and stacked in plastic bins. It's not *that* much work to stuff it into the back of my car; most of the work is going to be once I get to the convention center and try to set it all up. Olivia does most of the talking between us as we move stuff, since I'm still waiting for the triple-shot of espresso to hit my bloodstream and help me shake off my zombie brain.

"...and I'm just *dying* to have that conversation with Keller," Olivia sighs, as I open the passenger door of the car for her. "Please tell me he's gone chaotic good. He has, hasn't he? Just tell me out of character, *please,* and I promise I won't bug you about game for the whole rest of the day."

I shoot Olivia a sleepy smile as I settle into the driver's seat. "I like when you bug me about game," I tell her. "Bug away." I have to resist the urge to reach out and ruffle her hair. I force myself to start the car and put my hands safely on the wheel instead. "Okay, fine. Yes, Keller is officially chaotic good, as of last night's game. Good job, Elsinore."

Olivia gasps with unmitigated pleasure. "I'm so happy," she says. "This is the *best*. I had to work on that bastard for *two years*, but it was so worth it!"

*Absolutely worth it,* I think, as I shoot her a sideways glance. I put a lot of work into this particular sideplot, making sure the group had the chance to interact with the Prince of Thieves on a regular basis, giving Elsinore a bunch of chances to tempt him into mending his ways. I hadn't really been sure how I was going to exhibit Keller's final change of heart—but the moment that Elsinore went unconscious, I *knew* it was the perfect time to pull it off. The group's reaction—and Olivia's reaction, in particular—were everything I could have hoped for. I'm tired as hell this morning, but I just can't bring myself to care. I'm so glad I ran that session last night, if only to see how thrilled Olivia is this morning.

"You're sure you don't mind talking about game?" Olivia asks me worriedly. She's fidgeting with the edge of that loose-knit shirt, suddenly shy. "I know you've got a lot to worry about today."

I shake my head at her in disbelief. "It's *my* game!" I tell her. "I run it because I enjoy it! I love it when you guys get excited enough to ramble at me. It lets me know I'm doing a good job."

Olivia blushes lightly. "You're doing a *great* job," she corrects me. "I'm really having so much fun, Finn. I basically count down the days to each session."

I'm only a mortal man. That bra, this coffee, that little bit of ego-stroking... if I weren't driving this car, I'd be in big trouble. As it is, my brain is suddenly suggesting I find somewhere to stop so I can drag Liv over into my lap and kiss her senseless, and maybe find out what that lace feels like beneath my fingers...

"Okay," Olivia mumbles. "I... I have this idea I've been working on." She's staring down at her hands, biting at her lower lip—all but squirming with shyness now. "I didn't want to bring it up until I was sure Keller was going to change alignment, but... I've been working on a custom exalted class. Like, for reformed villains. It's totally not even play-tested, but I thought if you liked the class, and if it's not too much for the plot, maybe Keller could take a level or two in it?"

Clearly, it is Christmas in July, and I am on Santa's good list. I can't believe what I'm hearing. "You... you wrote your own exalted class?" I manage. "For my non-player character?"

Olivia bites down harder on her lip. "It's weird, I'm sorry," she says quickly. "It's not a serious thing, it was just an idea I had—"

"That's *amazing*, Liv," I reassure her. "You didn't know the first thing about T&T two years ago, and now you're writing your own classes!" I press my palm to my chest, feigning a choked voice. "I'm... I'm so *proud.*"

Olivia's little blush has now gone flaming red. "It's

probably unbalanced," she mumbles. "I mean, I tried to compare to a bunch of existing classes and take inspiration from their abilities, but I'm not, like, a professional or anything…"

"I'd *love* to see it," I tell her. "I'll help you workshop it if you want. Once you guys get your next level, I'll have Keller make the switch."

"Oh my god, really?" Olivia looks up at me, and those hazel eyes of her are all but shining with unmitigated bliss. "You are. You are just. The *best*."

I grin at the road ahead of me. *I am the best,* I think. *According to Liv, at least. I like that.* "I'm *so* glad you finally admitted it, Sparrow," I drawl, in the voice I normally use when I'm playing Keller. "And here I was beginning to think you were impossibly immune to my charms."

Olivia chokes on a surprised laugh. "Excuse me, Your Highness," she says back, elevating her tone to the one she uses when she plays Elsinore. "I said I was *quite* charmed, that time that you helped us hunt down the princess' assassin. I have always given credit where credit is due."

We pull into the parking lot of the convention center, and I grab an open parking spot. It's still ungodly early, so I'm able to find one conveniently right near the front entrance. I get out and head around to open Olivia's door for her, leaning slightly inside the car with my elbow resting on top.

"You are by far the hardest woman I have ever had to woo, Dame Elsinore," I sigh, as I look down at her. "Most ladies are happy to settle for trinkets. You are the first one I have ever met to insist I go *assassin-hunting*."

"Oh?" Olivia straightens in her seat. Her hazel eyes

sparkle up at me. Slowly, she pushes herself out of the car, standing up just within the circle of my arm. I can feel her heat again, just inches away from me. She's wearing a brighter, cheerier pink lipstick than usual, and I find myself wondering if it tastes like something fruity. "And *are* you trying to woo me, Your Highness?" she asks mischievously. "I find myself unclear on the subject."

*Uh.* I catch myself a bit too late. I hadn't intended on flirting with Olivia too overtly in-character—I have a rule about letting female players make the first move in game romances, just to be sure I'm not making them uncomfortable. But Liv doesn't seem at all uncomfortable right now. In fact, there's that same little crackle of heat between us that makes me wish even more deeply that I didn't have a whole room full of T&T games to organize in the next hour.

"*Was* I unclear?" I try to keep my voice light, but there's a sudden roughness there that I can't get a handle on. "I should remedy that. I am *absolutely* trying to woo you, little Sparrow. I have been, for the last two years." Olivia isn't breathing. I can tell, because her warm breath has stopped ghosting along my cheek. She stares up at me, her hazel eyes wide. I can't resist the urge anymore— I reach down to brush my thumb along her cheek. Her skin is deliciously soft. "Is it working?" I murmur.

Olivia swallows hard. Her eyes drop to my lips. Her cheeks are obviously flushed. "It is *so* working," she mumbles.

I lean over and cross that last inch, brushing my lips over hers. Olivia lets out a shocked whimper—but before I can wonder if I've misread the situation, she leans up on her toes, meeting my kiss. Her lips part shyly, and her tongue darts against mine. I let out a groan and lean against her, trapping her body against the car.

Her arms slide up around my back. Her body moulds against mine. I can feel her heart racing like a little trapped rabbit. Her breasts crush against my chest. Her legs part for me just a little bit, but I force myself not to take the invitation; I'm suddenly so hard it hurts, and the last thing I want to do is scare her off before I even get the chance to kiss her properly.

And I do. Kiss her properly, that is. I pull back just a bit, so I can nibble at the corner of her mouth. Liv lets out a soft, tiny moan, and I catch it against my mouth, running the tip of my tongue against the place where her lips part. She closes her teeth gently around my lower lip, surprising me—there's a hot, excited impatience in her next moan, and now I'm moving more quickly than I mean to.

I slide my hands into her chestnut hair, forcing her mouth more firmly against mine. Our tongues dance with rough desperation. Her sandalled foot brushes against the outside of my leg as she shifts to press herself fully against me, and *oh god*, I want to get this woman naked right here and now and screw her in the back seat of my car.

My phone rings.

Olivia blinks quickly, as though the sound has jerked her out of some dreamlike trance. She pulls away, with her cheeks flushed and her hair satisfyingly mussed. "Do... do you need to answer that?" she asks breathlessly.

"I do *not* need to answer that right now," I manage. I pull her mouth back to mine, and she lets out an adorable little squeak. Her fingers dig into my back, clenching in my shirt. Her foot travels just a bit further up the back of my leg, and I can feel her toes curling there. I've made her toes curl. I'm pretty sure that's a good thing.

Liv rubs herself against me with a soft mewl of pleasure, and a jolt of pure, molten *hunger* runs through me. I need to find the nearest horizontal surface, pronto, and see what other noises I can pry out of her.

My phone goes to voicemail. And then, god damn it, it rings *again.*

I'm about ready to grab the thing and dash it to pieces on the concrete, but Olivia shimmies out of my grip back into the car and fumbles around for the phone instead. I take a deep, steadying breath, counting down from ten. I am *not* in the right frame of mind to answer my phone right now. But Liv hands it over with a sheepish look on her face that suggests she thinks she's being helpful, and I take it from her with a mournful sigh.

"*Yes?*" I answer the phone, with a bit more snap in my voice than I probably intend. "What is so important?"

"*Uh. Oh god. I'm so sorry. It sounds like you're already having a rough morning.*" I freeze at the miserable-sounding voice on the other end of the phone. It's Lisa, one of my few female GMs for the day... and she's clearly not well. "*I am really, really sick. Like, tossing my guts in the toilet sick. I was hoping it was just food poisoning and it might clear up by this morning, but I just confirmed I'm running a fever, too.*"

I close my eyes and try to recenter myself. *I'm organizing a whole room full of tabletop games,* I remind myself. *That's what I'm here for. And now I'm down my last alternate GM.*

"Yeah, uh... *obviously* don't come to the convention if you're feeling like that," I tell her. "Look, stuff happens. It's why we have alternates."

"*I know,*" Lisa sighs. "*But I am the alternate. I feel so bad about this, Finn. Have you got someone else who can still run my table?*"

Olivia is giving me a concerned expression, and an only-slightly-crazy idea occurs to me. "Maybe," I say. "Look, don't worry about it either way, Lisa. It's not your problem. You focus on getting some electrolytes in you and rest up, okay?"

"*Okay,*" Lisa mumbles. "*Hey, my boyfriend's gonna be there, I'll have him bring my printed materials, if that helps?*"

"Your boyfriend's still coming?" I ask, bewildered. "He's not staying home to look after you?"

"*It's okay,*" Lisa assures me. "*I told him to go and have fun.*" It doesn't sound okay, but I force myself not to pry. Lisa's a nice woman, and her relationship is absolutely none of my business. "*Ugh, okay, I... I think I need to hurl again. I'll send my stuff up with Brian.*"

The phone call ends abruptly, and I slide it slowly into my jeans pocket.

"Is, uh. Is everything okay?" Olivia asks me. She's carefully not looking at me now, with her fingers twisted up in her knitted shirt. It occurs to me that I didn't get a chance to run my fingers over that bra of hers, and I can taste the disappointment on my tongue.

Still. I've got a room full of people waiting on me.

I take a breath. "Lisa's down for the count," I tell her. "I think she caught the same flu that Carter got. She was our last alternate, so we're down a table for two slots now."

Olivia's eyes widen. "Oh, shit," she breathes. "That's awful. Have you got anyone you can ask to take over last-second?"

I continue staring at her. Slowly—meaningfully—I raise my eyebrows.

Olivia's mouth drops open. "Oh," she says. "Oh no, Finn. I barely know how to play. I can't *run* a game! Especially not for a table full of strangers!"

I grin at her. "You barely know how to play?" I ask skeptically. "Miss *I-Just-Wrote-a-Custom-Exalted-Class?*"

Olivia closes her mouth again with a snap. Slowly, it seems to dawn on her that she's turned into a knowledge-able little geek, just like the rest of us. "Uh..." Liv blinks her way through that revelation. "Okay. I can probably fumble my way through the rules. But I still haven't ever been a GM before. I don't even know if I'll be any good at it."

I lean down to brush my lips over hers again. It's good. It's natural. She *does* taste like something fruity. I think it might be strawberries, but I'll need a few more licks to be sure.

"You," I tell her softly, "would be a perfectly good gamemaster. You care about making sure everyone has fun. And that's the most important part."

Her hazel eyes stare up at me, slightly glazed. I realize I'm being a little bit unfair, springing this on her right after that kiss.

"It's okay," I say quickly, reversing course. "It's a lot to ask at the last second. I can ask around at the con, and find someone else—"

"No!" Olivia straightens suddenly. "No, I can do it. I

said I wanted to help out today. You need help. So I'll help."

I didn't think I could possibly be any more attracted to this woman. But god help me, that's the sexiest thing she's said all morning.

5

———

**OLIVIA**

*W*hat the hell have I gotten myself into?

I glance across the large ballroom the convention uses for its official society tabletops, searching out Finn's figure. He's rushing around—checking on GMs, handing out adventure packets, making sure everyone's got a bottled water next to them. I'm exhausted just *watching* him.

I'm also unbearably turned on. That *kiss*. Holy hell. I didn't know kisses like that happened in real life. Somehow, we went from intense, geeky game discussion to cheerful half-roleplayed banter to... *that*. I can't help the way my eyes linger on those tight jeans of his, or the way my legs cross uncomfortably, thinking of the way he was pressed between my thighs. I was absolutely ready to drag him into that car and have my way with him, and I'm pretty sure he was thinking the same crazy thoughts. If Lisa hadn't called in sick, in fact, I am one hundred percent positive that I would have slept with Finn O'Roarke by now.

*I hate the flu,* I think miserably. *I can't hate Lisa, so I really,* really *hate the flu.*

We haven't even had time to talk about what just happened. I know that conversation's coming—and I'm half-excited for it, half-dreading it. Once Finn and I have both cooled down, there's not really any guarantee that there's going to be a relationship there. I mean, god, I want to *hope* there is, but until we actually sit down and discuss like adults, I just can't be sure.

"Hey," Finn asks breathlessly. His hand comes down lightly on my shoulder and squeezes, and I look up to find him standing next to my table. "You're sure you're still good to do this?"

I know my face is flaming crimson again. Just that little touch is enough to bring back the whole memory of that kiss against the car. "Yeah," I manage, though my voice comes out in a squeak. "Yeah, I'm good." I clear my throat roughly. "I looked through the adventure packet. It's nice and short and clear. It's just a first-level game; I'm pretty sure I can handle it."

Finn shoots me a relieved smile. "You're a good woman, Sparrow," he mumbles to me. His fingers tighten on my shoulder, and he leans down to brush my lips with his again. It's a soft, reassuring kiss—but I'm still shocked that he does it in the middle of the convention. Mild PDA like that is far from off-limits, but oh my god, that means this is a *thing*. We're a thing.

A wobbly, indistinct, kind of *questionable* thing—but still a thing.

Finn smiles gently at me as he pulls back, and my heart flutters giddily. "We're stuck here 'till eight," he says apologetically. "But... I'd like to talk after cleanup. I'd really... *really* like that."

I dare to reach up and grab his hand. I squeeze it lightly, with a shy smile. "Yeah. I'd like that too.'

"Finn!" someone yells from across the room. "Doors open in five!"

Finn hesitates. Then, he brings my hand up to his lips and presses a quick kiss against my palm. "You're gonna do great," he promises me. He lets me go grudgingly and slides a piece of paper onto the table in front of me. "I got you registered as a society gamemaster. You should be good to go. Just make sure all your players write down your GM number at the start of game. I'll come help you sign off on their sheets at the end of game."

I've got a silly grin on my face as I look up at him. I don't care. I'd run a hundred terrifying, twentieth-level games for another little kiss on my palm like that. But I don't have to—all I have is this first-level game today, and another one tomorrow.

Finn shoots me a wink. "Don't torture anyone *too* badly," he says.

I roll my eyes. "First-level characters can't endure much torture," I reply. "A bad enough *rat bite* can kill them."

I can still hear the tail-end of Finn's low chuckle as he strides away toward the person that called his name. I let my gaze linger on him just a little while longer, before I turn my attention back to the table in front of me.

Five more minutes, and I'll be a gamemaster.

* * *

The doors open soon enough. A bunch of excited players stream in, all raring to go. It's a funny sight this early in the morning, compared to the pitiful people who normally drag themselves into the coffee shop begging for their morning cup of joe, but I've noticed that TowerCon tends to incite that kind of bubbly energy in people.

Almost instantly, I've got my own table full of players —most of them were waiting impatiently outside the doors while we finished our setup. I've got two teen boys at my table—surprisingly polite, given what I remember from being a teenager—along with their dad. There's also a very sleepy man in a button-down shirt and glasses, and a huge, bear-like guy that reminds me fondly of Samson.

I launch into the neat little checklist in front of me, but I barely need to bother—everyone here knows how society works, and they're basically doing my job for me before I can even instruct them. Everyone's already got my GM number down on their record sheet for the game, and they're writing their names and pronouns on their little paper placards. I start writing down everyone's race, class, and character names for my own notes.

It's a generally positive atmosphere in here, which buoys my confidence. I can see Finn sitting down with his first group—this year's lottery winners, deeply enthused to be at his table. Finn has his gamemaster face on, and I can tell just from his body language that he's already started setting the first scene. I smile stupidly, and turn back toward my own group.

I'm running the same module both today and tomorrow, just to make things easier. I haven't played it before

—but the story is straightforward, and the stats are all incredibly simple.

The father at my table is dutifully playing a cleric of Hirtel, god of mercy, so that he can heal his sons' characters, and I can't help but find that painfully cute. His two sons have brought a ranger character and a wizard character to the table, and they've decided they're *also* brothers in-game. The family dynamic catches on, and soon enough, our rogue in the glasses and our bear-like fighter both decide that they're playing the teens' uncles.

"Don't you dare shoot me in the back again!" the wizard teen grumbles to his ranger brother, as they get into a fight with some zombies. "Aim that bow at the zombie *over there*."

"I'm sure he's fine," the rogue in the glasses assures the wizard. "I've been helping him practice. He only shot me once last time!"

"And this is why I need a god's help to keep my family alive," the father sighs heavily. "I go heal my brother this turn."

"Which one?" I ask, bemused.

"The one with the zombie bite in his shoulder," he replies wryly, pointing at the fighter.

It's just a first-level game, but I feel like I'm walking on cloud nine. My group is having so much fun, and I'm having fun *with* them. Every scene is just hilarious, with them bickering back and forth like a real family. We reach the end of the scenario far faster than I'd like, and I can tell that everyone's a little disappointed to be done. Then, right in front of me, the players at my table start exchanging email addresses and phone numbers, and I'm watching a regular T&T group form right before my eyes.

"Well, that just leaves us in need of a GM," the father notes. He glances over at me with a smile. "I don't guess you're available on Wednesday nights?"

I blush furiously. I'm so touched, I have to struggle to find words. "I... I'm afraid I'm not," I admit. "But I'm so glad you guys enjoyed yourselves that much. You really liked the game?"

"We *loved* it," the ranger kid tells me. "Dude, that little scream you did for the necromancer, when I shot him in the knee—" He cuts off into an approximation of the high-pitched shriek I made, and the whole table devolves into laughter again.

"You need any help with your end-of-game logistics, Liv?" I turn around and see Finn standing just behind my chair. He's got this soft, knowing smile on his face, and I know he caught the tail-end of that conversation.

"Uh... no, I think we're actually pretty good," I tell him. "Everyone here knows what they're doing even better than I do."

"Pshaw, you're fine," the rogue assures me. He blinks at Finn's con badge and brightens up suddenly. "Hey, you're Finn O'Roarke! I didn't realize you were a guest this year!"

Finn reaches out to shake his hand. "I'm a guest every year," he says with a grin. "At least at *this* con. It's a short enough drive for me."

"Are you busy?" the rogue asks. "I don't guess you'd mind signing a gaming book for me?"

"Nah, not at all." Finn searches out a pen behind my GM's screen. The rogue digs in his bag and hands over a battered old copy of *Infernal Villains*, another one of Finn's more popular books. "You up for lunch, Liv?" Finn asks me, as he scribbles a quick signature. "I've got a breather before I have to start my next game. I want to hear all about how your first game went."

The high from my first successful game gets even higher. It's... kind of like a date. A really super quick date, given that Finn's got to run back to organizing within the hour, but *still*. "I'd love that," I gush. "Oh man, it was great, Finn—I've got *stories*."

Finn's eyes meet mine, and I can see the same excitement inside me mirrored behind them. This is how Finn must feel *all the time*, whenever he runs our games. He's not just being polite, asking about my game. He really does want to know every little detail. "I can't wait," he says sincerely. He offers me a hand up, and I take it. That spark between us is burning like a bonfire now. I thought I was attracted to him before, but I really had no idea. There's something really special about being able to share the experience of GMing with Finn, knowing that he understands exactly how I'm feeling right now.

"*Fantastic* game," says the dad at my table. "Thank you so much for running for my kids." He shakes my hand before they head off, and the other players follow suit.

Finn bumps his shoulder into mine, as we start walking for the door outside. "Looks like you did a good job," he teases me.

"They really made it easy for me," I admit. "They decided to play a whole *family*, Finn—it was hilarious. I've never seen a group click so quickly before."

Finn reaches out to snag my hand in his. It startles me —and then, it warms me. I curl my fingers tightly around his, savoring the feel of it. "What classes were they playing?" he asks.

Before I know it, I've launched into a blow-by-blow recounting of the whole game. We reach the sandwich place partway through. The guys at the counter are nice enough to jump us through the line when they see we've got GM badges, since they know we've got events to run, so we're able to settle in at a table in short order.

It's the same place we ate at two years ago, when I first met Finn. It feels kind of karmic, somehow. He loops his arm around my waist as we talk, so I'm able to snuggle under his arm. He's still listening to my game stories with rapt attention, and I don't know if I could possibly be happier.

Before I know it, we're five minutes until Finn has to get back. We both hurry to finish off our food, and it only occurs to me as he's heading off that I just spent all lunch talking about my *game*, instead of about *us*.

*Oh, shit,* I think with a wince. As fun as our chat was, that means I definitely have to wait for tonight after clean-up just to get some closure. I'm done with the one game I was supposed to run today, but Finn's booked for the whole rest of the day. I'm going to drive myself *insane* in the meantime.

Just as I'm thinking this, Finn gets up out of the booth and turns to take my hand. His lips brush over the back of my fingers, and I grin like a moron. His brown eyes sparkle at me.

"I am *very* impressed with your storytelling skills right now," he tells me.

Okay, I'll admit it. This is almost as good as having sex in the back seat of his car. *Almost.*

"I learned from the best," I tell him, with an arched eyebrow.

Finn smiles at that—and the way his eyes crinkle at the edges just makes my heart flip-flop in my chest.

Now I know I've got it bad for him. B-A-D, with super extra emphasis. If I don't end this day with both of us naked, I think I might just explode from hormones.

"Have a great con, Liv," Finn tells me, with another kiss on my hand. "I can't wait to see you tonight."

That's definitely a good indication we're headed in the right direction.

I shove to my feet and press my mouth against his. Finn freezes in surprise for a second—but then, he lifts his hands up to press them against my cheeks, and he kisses me back with the kind of slightly-indecent hunger that doesn't belong in a sandwich shop in the middle of the day. His tongue dives between my lips, twisting roughly with mine. The back of my knees bump up against the booth, and I'm holding onto him for dear life, with electric shivers of attraction jumping up and down my spine.

Finn forces himself to pull away—but he's breathing hard, and his eyes are dark as he looks down at me. "*Please* remind me that I need to go be a responsible adult right now," he begs me.

I have to blink a few times to clear my head. My whole body is hot again, and I *desperately* want to feel his hands on me. But I force my mouth to work again. "You. Um." *Brain. Start working again, please.* I take a deep breath, slide my arms around his neck, and lean in toward his ear.

"I'll hold that thought until tonight, Your Highness," I whisper there, in a breathy, suggestive tone.

There's an *instant* reaction against me, and I can't help but grin.

"Oh, *hell*," Finn mumbles. His eyes are slightly glazed over at the idea. "Yes, please."

I wriggle out of his arms. There's a brief, tortured disappointment on Finn's face that makes me laugh. "Go be an adult," I tell him helpfully.

"Only if I *have* to," he mutters.

Finn gives me one last tragic look, before heading back for the convention center.

## 6

## FINN

*I*'d like to say I give my games the full attention they deserve, but I'm not going to lie: I am a *very* distracted man.

I'm not imagining things, am I? I've just been promised a very *enthusiastic* night with the woman I've been pining after for two years. I'm pretty sure that just happened.

The clock on my phone seems to tick by with *interminable* slowness. Every time the players at my table get to roleplaying with each other, I find myself replaying that husky whisper in my head. This inevitably leads me to imagining what might have happened if I *hadn't* been such a responsible adult. I could have dragged Liv to my hotel room. I could have peeled off that lacy bra of hers and made her scream for me—

"It's the villain's turn, I think?" one of my players says to me, and I have to tear myself free of some very naughty thoughts.

"Yes!" I manage. "Yes, it is. And he's identified the

weak spot in your group, I'm afraid. He starts chanting a dark spell. Cold shadows slither up from the floor around him, coalescing around his hands. You have just enough time to recognize the spell as *Withering Hand* before those shadows hurtle toward your sorcerer. Make a constitution save, please."

The whole party groans—but it's probably my villain's last round still breathing, and I want to make sure he does some damage before he goes down. The sorcerer predictably fails his save, since he's used his constitution as a dump stat. He goes down to negatives instantly, though I intentionally miscount the damage on the dice to make sure I don't kill him outright. I'm in an unusually generous mood, for reasons I'm sure I don't need to elucidate.

My last game finishes up, and I'm more tightly-wound than ever. I have a few handshakes and a few nice words with my players. But I can't possibly be more relieved to see people clearing off their tables and ambling for the doors.

I unlock my phone to call Olivia—but there's already a message waiting for me there.

***OLIVIA: Dinner?***

I'm terribly torn. On the one hand, I could use more food in my stomach. On the other hand—I'm *incredibly* peopled-out for the day. And I'm gonna be honest, I'm looking forward to getting Olivia alone for a bit.

***FINN: How about room service?***

I second-guess the text almost as soon as I've sent it. There's not much context—what if she takes it as a come-on? I mean... it *is* a little bit of a come-on. But maybe it's too much, too quickly? Ugh, I can't take it back now. Maybe I ought to qualify it with another text.

Another text comes in just as I'm typing.

**OLIVIA: Sounds great.**

I blink down at the screen a few times, just to make sure I've read it properly.

*This is happening,* I think. *Holy shit.*

I'm so thrown by the realization that I nearly walk right past the subject of my thoughts as I leave the ballroom. Olivia is standing off to one side near the doors, with her phone in her hand. She's smiling at her screen with an expression I've never seen on her face before. It's a secret, deeply-pleased little quirk of her pink-tinted lips, like she's just done something naughty and doesn't regret it a single bit.

How can I resist a smile like that?

I snag her around the waist, and Olivia startles, looking up at me. Her hazel eyes meet mine, and those pink lips part in breathless anticipation.

I've really been intending to have a sit-down chat with her all day—to make sure we're both on the same page relationship-wise, to make sure she knows I'm interested in something serious. But Liv's tongue darts out to lick at her lower lip, and I find I absolutely have to lean down and follow her lead. I take a taste of my own, savoring the lingering bit of strawberry there. She lets out a soft, encouraging moan. Her fingers come up to knot in my shirt, as though she could drag me even closer than I already am.

Somehow, I force myself to pull away. There's a hotel room just a block away with a lot more privacy, if I can make it there. "I'm going a little crazy," I admit against her lips. I remember that naughty smile she had before, and I decide to throw caution to the wind. "I'm going to do *such* bad things to you, Liv."

She's already flushed and breathing hard. But I swear I can see her toes curl in her sandals as I say the words. "Ohgod," Olivia manages. "Yes, *please.*"

Every other thought gets roughly shoved aside at that.

Room service can wait.


**OLIVIA**

My heart is going a mile a minute when that text message shows up on my phone. *Room service.* I was expecting we'd be painfully mature about this whole thing—maybe go talk over drinks, do our due diligence, and *then*, if I'm lucky, end up somewhere private to finish what we started this morning. But we're skipping straight to the fun part, and that revelation sends a zing of heat right down between my legs.

When Finn actually catches up with me and kisses me and tells me he's going to do *very bad things* to me, I'm pretty sure I can hear choirs of angels singing in my head. I'm not hungry anymore. Or rather—I'm hungry for something that has *nothing* to do with food.

We head across the street to the hotel where most of the con-goers are staying. Finn always has a room, even though his house is relatively close by. He told me once that he always crashes by the end of the first day, and the extra hour or so of sleep before day two makes a huge difference. I am *positive* we don't intend to sleep just yet. Probably not for a while. *Hopefully* not for a while.

We're packed into an elevator with a bunch of other

chatty attendees, all going to different floors. Finn has me tucked back against him. His fingers are hot, stroking just beneath my knitted top. By the time we get to his floor, my knees are wobbling, and my panties are wet.

Then—*finally*—we're stumbling through the door of Finn's hotel room, and his lips are hot and hungry on mine, and I know we don't have to stop.

He lifts my top up over my head, tossing it aside. The air conditioning is turned up in here, and it makes me shiver as it hits my bare skin—but Finn presses me up against the wall, and his heat immediately makes up for the absence. His lips trace down my neck, lingering on the strap of my bralette... then he's moving further down, darting his tongue out to taste the swell of my breast, just over the lace that covers it. I've got my fingers clenched in his dark hair, urging him on, begging him to keep going. I'm simultaneously thrumming with heat and clouded by incredulity. It doesn't seem *real* that we're doing this. It's almost too good, too dreamlike. I'm expecting to wake up at any moment.

I claw at Finn's shirt with trembling hands, desperate to get my palms on his naked skin. He breaks away just long enough to shrug off his t-shirt, and I get to see where that dark hair curls on his chest, trailing its way down below the waistband of his jeans. I've got the most shocking impulse to lick my way down that line of hair to see where it goes—but his mouth is on mine again, and his hot skin rubs against my nipples through my bra. It's like an appetizer before dinner: it's not *nearly* enough, but it gives me the strength to hold on just a little bit longer.

Then, Finn's fingers undo the button of my slacks, and his hand slides down the front. The very tip of his finger rubs against my wetness, and I buck against him with a shocked moan of pleasure.

*Now.* Now this feels real.

Finn swallows up my moan with his mouth. He circles my slit with his fingertip, then dips it slowly inside me. A groan vibrates through him as he realizes just how slick I already am.

I'm going to combust. Seriously: I'm going to catch on fire right here and now, if I don't get him inside me. No spell resistance, no saving throw—just sheer fiery death from lack of Finn.

I'm out of patience. I shove at the waistband of my pants and my panties, wriggling them down my legs so that they pool on the floor. I fumble with his jeans, but I'm lousy with the zipper. If I was in a different frame of mind, I might find it funny. I'm trying to take off Finn's pants right now, and I'm doing an awful job of it. That's hilarious.

Finn takes a moment to help me slide his jeans down just far enough, and his cock springs free, and I am *definitely* not laughing now. He's raging hard, which makes it easy to see the whole glorious length of him. He's big and thick, and I'm wondering for just a second whether he's going to fit inside me. At the same time, I *desperately* want to try.

I slide one leg eagerly up his, making it easier for him to settle between my legs. I feel him harden even further, as his tip presses into my wetness. Finn lets out a hiss of pure, existential frustration though, and he presses his forehead into my shoulder.

"I don't have any protection," he mumbles. "Where the hell is my head at—"

I can't help the embarrassed laugh that trickles out of me. "I have some protection," I manage. "I, um. Bought some." *Today.* At the pharmacy around the corner. Wearing my con badge and all. The lady behind the counter gave me a raised eyebrow that suggested she thought I was going to be having some kind of kinky elf sex tonight.

I rummage through my pants on the floor and pull out the condom I stashed in my pocket. I would normally just *die* of embarrassment revealing that I have it in front of Finn, but right now is a very different matter. He grabs it from me and shoves me back onto the hotel bed with a suddenness that makes me squeal.

"Foresight is a *very* attractive quality in a woman, Sparrow," Finn breathes against me, as he slides his body on top of mine. The nickname sends an electric shock through me, as though he'd reached out and stroked my clit. No one's ever given me a nickname before, and this one comes with a hundred oddly-intense little memories from the last two years. Finn's voice is low and raspy, and it makes the sound of it just that much sexier.

He's hot and mostly-naked, with his jeans riding low on his hips and his cock hard with impatience. Finn tears open the condom and rolls it onto his length. I'm a little bit relieved that it fits.

Then, he's pushing slowly inside me, and I might just combust anyway.

I can feel every inch of him as he stretches me out, bit by bit. I startle myself with a very loud, very emphatic *yes* that seems to fill the whole room. Finn grins at that, and it has a devastating effect on me. His eyes are dark and hungry, and when he sheathes himself fully inside me, he lets out an equally loud, approving groan.

I writhe underneath him, trying to find some way to take more of him in. This feels so good, so *right*. He rolls his hips, thrusting into me again, and I lose what little breath I have. Finn's fingers tangle in my hair, pulling it loose from its ponytail so that the tie stops digging uncomfortably into the back of my head—and strangely, it's that thoughtful, casual intimacy that finally convinces me we're not just friends anymore. Friends don't helpfully undo your ponytail during sex. That's definitely a lovers sort of thing.

God, I'm weird. It's a good thing Finn is into weird.

I wrap my legs around his waist, needing him closer, deeper, faster. It doesn't actually do much to make things easier, but his cock twitches when my ankles lock behind his back, and I can tell it's turning him on harder. He breathes my name against my mouth—and I nearly come, just from the way he makes it sound. Never in a hundred years would I imagine Finn saying my name like that. I want to hear it again and again.

I try to tell him as much—but all that comes out of my mouth is "please, please, please, oh god, *yes*" which is, I guess, almost as good.

"Oh, fuck, *Liv*," he moans, as he slides into me again. It's a startling word from his mouth. Finn is always so careful to be nice and approachable. I know he knows how to swear, but it's like he saves it for special occasions. I'm a special occasion, apparently. I decide I like that too.

I raise my hips to meet him on the next thrust, taking him deeper. It's a blissful sensation, edged with just a little pain. I *can* take him that deep, but only barely. I still enjoy it, so I do it again, the next time he slams into me. I'm going to have some very weird, very satisfying bruises tomorrow.

The next thrust nearly takes us both off the side of the bed. We never made it to the pillows, and we've been so enthusiastic that I seem to have crept back too far. There's an awkward moment where Finn chokes on laughter, and we both have to wiggle around in the proper direction. As I settle back into a pillow this time, he presses his elbow next to my head and kisses me, still laughing. The wry smile on his face melts my heart, and *oh no*, I'm pretty sure I'm actually in love.

"Take two?" Finn mumbles against my mouth. The corners of his lips twitch against mine. *Nngh.* I think my ovaries just imploded from sheer sweetness.

"I can't count that high right now," I tell him dazedly. "Uhm. Keep going."

Finn obliges with another thrust that sinks me down into the pillows. This one hits a particularly good spot, and I arch my neck with a loud whimper. Sexy, perceptive, amazing Finn has of course noticed this change in pitch—so he hits it again. Warm tingles start swimming up my spine, and I know I'm getting close to coming.

His lips brush along my cheek, moving toward my ear. "Gonna come for me, Liv?" Finn asks in a hot whisper.

He hits that spot one more time, and I answer with a strangled, incoherent cry. The warmth that was building inside me overwhelms my nerves in a blissful rush. I cling to him while I come, tightening on his cock. Finn pauses to stare down at me, his brown eyes locked on my face with rapt attention. As the waves of pleasure slowly come and go, he brushes my hair back from my face and kisses my mouth more gently than before. I feel unexpectedly, unbearably cared for. Like he thinks I'm something precious and valuable.

I melt like a candle. I don't know what I was expecting tonight, exactly, but this has blown me away. I want more of it. I want this *every night*, and I don't care how selfish that sounds. "Oh god, *Finn*," I sigh. "This is... this is really..."

"Mmhm," he agrees against my mouth. Finn moves again, and I realize he's been holding back while I catch my breath. It occurs to me that I'd really like to repay the favor and blow his mind in return.

I shove at Finn's shoulder, and he blinks. As I shove again, he realizes what I'm after, and he lets me roll him over beneath me. His hands settle on my hips, and I'm treated to the sight of him looking up at me with those dark, hungry eyes.

I lean in and pull his earlobe slowly between my lips. Finn shivers obediently, and I grin. "I've been wanting to do this for a while now, Your Highness," I murmur there, in the most sultry tone I can manage.

His cock twitches inside me, and I know I've hit paydirt.

I rotate my hips lightly, to generate a bit more friction. "I'll admit," I breathe. "I have a *thing* for scoundrels. You always get me so wet... and frustrated." I punctuate the statement with a roll of my hips, taking him in deep again.

Finn lets his head fall back with a loud, surprised moan. I'm pretty sure I've shocked him into some kind of naughty bliss. It's good to know I'm not the only one with some unresolved sexual tension to work out between our characters.

"I'm gonna die," Finn mumbles, with a glazed look in his eyes. "You're gonna kill me, Sparrow."

The nickname sends another shiver through me. I might be super embarrassed about this tomorrow—but for now, it's the hottest thing I've ever done.

I move my hips, riding him slowly while I kiss the place just next to his ear. "Did you get hurt in that fight?" I murmur with a grin. The next lazy shimmy of my hips makes his fingers tighten on my skin. "I suppose, since you've been *such* a gentleman lately... I could see about kissing it better."

His hands still my hips, holding me firmly in place. Finn arches up off the bed with a loud, surprised *oh fuck*, and then he's coming inside me.

His breath jerks in his chest a few times—and then, he's dragged me down against him, wrapping his arms around me. "Ohhhhkay," he manages. "Wow." Then, after another pause: "Wow."

I can't help the proud, silly smile that spreads across my lips. I'm fairly sure I've accomplished my goal of blowing Finn's mind.

"I am *never* going to be able to unhear that," Finn mumbles. It sounds both pleased and guilty. "You are going to *slay* me at game from now on."

"I guess you'll have to work it off afterward somehow," I say innocently.

He lets out a breath against my hair. "Yeah. Yep. I think I'm gonna have to do that." Finn tightens his arms on me. "Liv?"

I blink sleepily against him. "Hm?"

"We should… go on a date," he says. "And do… dating things." He pauses, clearly struggling to unscramble his thoughts. "I'd like to date you, is what I'm getting at."

I grin and snuggle into his arms. "I'm glad you clarified that," I tease. "I wasn't sure that was what you meant when you said *go on a date*." My chest is warm though, and I'm so happy I could burst. "Today was pretty fun, though. I feel like it was date-worthy."

Finn chuckles, though there's a hint of relief in it. "Packing up stuff at six in the morning and sitting at different tables all day running games was a date?"

"I mean… *I* had fun." I smile dreamily. "Didn't you?"

Finn's fingers stroke my shoulder idly, and I decide I can *definitely* get used to this. "Yeah," he murmurs. "I really did."

## 7

## FINN

*W*e manage to find the energy for a leisurely shower and some room service. It's still relatively early in the evening for a convention, but we're both pretty exhausted. Post-game exhaustion is worlds better with Liv hanging out with me though, and there's something incredibly satisfying about lounging around naked with her, eating hotel ice cream and swapping stories about our games.

As it gets later in the evening, I get the chance to run my hands all over her again—properly, this time, now that we've released a little tension. I thought I'd learned all of Liv's pleased little sounds earlier, but kissing my way up the inside of her thigh and burying my head between her legs elicits brand new ones. I'm proud to say I leave her a *much* less eloquent wreck of a woman this time around, when she tumbles back into my arms and falls asleep.

I'm awake just a little bit longer than she is, as my

brain tries to process. I should be all over the place, based on previous experience—but I'm not. We've been friends for a while now. After today, I feel like we're on track to be *best* friends, as soon as we're able to make room in our lives for each other. I like the idea of spending every night with my best friend.

I've got the strangest certainty that I'm in love—that I'm holding the woman I want to marry, as soon as it's halfway reasonable to propose that sort of thing. I thread my fingers through hers, chewing on the idea of a ring on her finger. Olivia squeezes my hand back instinctively, blissfully unaware of my thoughts.

* * *

I wake up a lot less pleased than I fell asleep.

There's an alarm blaring insistently in my ears. I'm warm and comfortable, and I've got a soft woman in my arms, and I know I need to find my phone and destroy it for its impertinence.

Olivia's already awake, smiling sleepily at me. It takes my brain an extra moment to realize she's probably unfazed by the hour. That's really, terribly unfair. But I like waking up to that smile, so at least that dims the agony somewhat.

Olivia climbs over my body to flick off my phone's alarm, and I relax with a relieved sigh. But she keeps climbing, leaving the bed, and I'm not as pleased by that. I reach out to snatch at her waist, but Olivia shimmies away from me with a laugh.

"We've got games to run, Finn," she reminds me. "You're the one who scheduled them."

*Ugh.* I hate Past Me. "That's because I'm stupid," I mumble. "I shouldn't have done that."

Olivia leans down to brush her lips over mine, still smiling. "Crawl out of bed, and I'll find you some coffee," she promises.

My eyes sweep up and down her naked body. I check the clock mournfully, noting that there's not nearly enough time for a *different* pick-me-up. Caffeine will just have to do.

Olivia grins. "You're adorable when you're grumpy," she says.

I narrow my eyes at her and stumble out of bed after her. "I'm not adorable," I grumble. "*You're* adorable."

Olivia beams at me and plucks her pants from the floor. I don't want her putting on those pants. But I let her tug them on anyway, with the internal promise that I'll peel them right off her again tonight when we're done.

She cuddles into my side as we make our way back to the ballroom for the second day of games. By the time we're set up again, I've had *two* coffees, and plenty of stolen kisses, and I'm feeling much better about the whole day.


## OLIVIA

I feel like my feet haven't touched the ground once this morning.

Finn is back in organizer mode—and I have to admit, some part of me enjoys watching him run around making things happen—but he keeps dropping by to grab another sip of his coffee and just-one-more kiss. *For fuel,* he tells me seriously.

We're technically dating now, aren't we? We kind of decided yesterday was a date. That means my boyfriend keeps dropping by to kiss me. I grin at the idea, as I start digging out my own materials for game and setting up.

My phone dings softly, and I flip it on. I sent a quick text to Emily yesterday, letting her know I'd be staying with Finn instead of in the hotel room she's grabbed with Samson and Jim. I didn't have much time to check my replies after that, so there's a whole slew of them waiting for me now.

*EMILY: What do you mean by STAYING WITH FINN.*

*EMILY: I need clarification, Liv.*

*EMILY: LIV YOU ARE KILLING ME.*

The latest one is the one that she just sent me.

*EMILY: You owe me details.*

I snort and type out a quick reply.

*OLIVIA: Later, I'm about to run a game.*

And I really am. Just as I send off the text, the doors open, and our players filter inside in a repetition of yesterday's stampede.

It's not long before my first player reaches the table. She's short and cute, with friendly, rounded cheeks and a blond pixie haircut speckled with pink highlights. Her eyes light up as she finds my table number, and she heads over to hold out her hand. "Hi!" she says, suddenly even more enthusiastic. "I'm Ginny! I didn't realize I had a female GM, that's *great*—" She cuts herself off in embarrassment as I take her hand. "Oh, okay, that came out kind of weird. It's just that I got the impression there weren't many girls who played. I was expecting to be surrounded by tons of guys today, but I've already seen at least a few women."

"Hey Ginny," I greet her. "Nice to meet you. I'm Liv. And yeah, if you're at table four, I'm your GM today." I consider her curiously as I release her hand. "Are you new to the convention?"

"I'm new to the *game*," Ginny laughs. "I live nearby. I keep seeing all these people in crazy costumes walking around every year, and I finally decided I had to see what it was all about. I had to work yesterday, so I could only manage a Sunday badge."

I feel a sudden surge of nervousness at that. I have a brand new player? What if I'm not what she's expecting? What if I'm *terrible*, and she decides she never wants to play again, just because I'm inexperienced? I almost open my mouth to warn Ginny that it's my first weekend running... but I stop myself with a heavy breath. *I'll be fine,* I reassure myself. *It's the exact same first-level adventure. I've got this.*

"Well, I'm looking forward to running for you!" I tell her instead. "Here, I've got some pre-made characters you can look through. Do you have a preference?"

Ginny purses her lips, looking down at the pile of characters at the center of the table. She sifts through them with concentration. "Have you got an elf?' she asks. "I *love* those elf ears some of the cosplayers are wearing."

I grin. "You can wear elf ears even if you don't have an elven character," I promise her. "I think they have some in the dealer's room. But if you want, I think there's an elven druid in there."

Ginny separates out the druid with a small *aha!* "Cool," she says. "I get to pick a name?"

I'm feeling the weirdest sense of déjà vu right now. I nod at her slowly. "Yeah," I say. "You get to pick a name."

"Huh," Ginny mumbles. "I'm just realizing the only elf names I know are from *Lord of the Rings*. I definitely can't play a Legolas." She scrunches up her nose. "Do you think anyone would get mad at me if I played a druid named Celeborn? It's technically a guy name, but I've always liked the sound of it."

I have no idea who Celeborn is. I just nod enthusiastically. "Everyone's pretty friendly here," I assure her. "I don't think anyone will mind."

Ginny settles in at the table with her character sheet, in the seat closest to my GM screen. She nabs a pencil and writes the name *Celeborn* in fancy lettering at the top of her sheet.

"Woah! Fancy meeting *you* here, Dame Elsinore!" I look up at the voice and grin. Luke, the evil priest from my very first game, is standing at the edge of my table with a small folder and a set of dice. "Look at you, all grown up and running your own games!" He mimes wiping a proud tear from the corner of his eye.

"You're in another first-level game?" I ask him. "Did your priest die?"

"Oh no, never," Luke assures me. "He's far too selfish to die." He winks at me. "That character's gotten too high-level for most of the tabletops this weekend. I thought I'd start a lawful evil swashbuckler instead."

I goggle at him. "What *is* it with you and evil characters?" I ask. "You're so... *nice!*"

Luke slides in next to Ginny with a quick nod her way. "Oh, my dear pure Elsinore," he sighs. "I used to work in customer service. I needed *some* sort of outlet for my incoherent misanthropy." He pats the character in front of him. "Lawful evil is an *improvement*. I'm actually a recovering chaotic evil addict. Maybe if I play in a few more games of yours, I'll manage to make it to lawful neutral."

I cover a giggle. "Okay," I acknowledge. "Fair enough. Ginny here is new, so be a little gentle with her druid, huh?"

Luke grins at Ginny. "Always," he promises. "I had to get special dispensation to play evil characters in society games, you know. I swore up and down I'd never let it badly impact anyone at the table."

Ginny gives Luke a puzzled look. "You can *choose* to play an evil character?" she asks. "But wouldn't that make you a villain?"

"I prefer the term *antihero,*" Luke says, with an elegant wave of his hand. "The way I see it, alignment just represents how far you're willing to go to achieve your ends. Evil people can still have friends and play by the rules, when it makes sense for them to do so."

Ginny looks *fascinated* by this explanation. "So you're not, like... *Breaking Bad?*"

"More like a really early Tony Stark," Luke muses. "You know, when he was still a merchant of death type."

They devolve into an in-depth discussion of the alignment charts, and where Tony Stark actually falls on the grid. I'm actually really interested to hear where they go with it, but I have to get up and greet my other players as they arrive. The rest of our table is still guys, which isn't a huge surprise. But as I look around the ballroom, I can see more variation in the crowd than ever before. And I know Emily will be showing up later today, with Samson and Jim in tow.

"All right," I say. "Nice to meet you guys again. I'm Liv,

and I'm going to be running *The Village of Gimlet* for you today. This is a first-level game, so you should all have brand new characters. If you don't mind, I'd like us to go around the table and introduce our characters, and make sure everyone knows each other's pronouns." It's the same general script I ran through yesterday. The pronoun introductions are a new standard policy that the society just implemented last year, to make sure transgender and non-binary players feel welcome at the table. I haven't been in a game with either one yet, but Finn told me a few people emailed him after last year's con to tell him how much they appreciated the gesture.

I take note of my group's general makeup as we go around the circle. We've got Luke's swashbuckler, Ginny's druid, a fighter from the pre-gen pool, a custom-made warlock, and a first-level cleric. The last one gives me pause for more reasons than one.

"You're playing a cleric of Luin?" I ask the player. It's loud in here, and I can't be totally sure I've heard him correctly.

"I am!" he declares, with a lopsided smile. "I wanted to try something different for the con." He's an older guy —slim and well-groomed, with a black button-down and a salt-and-pepper beard. I look down at the paper placard in front of him again. He's written the name *Hero* where his player name should be, and I guess it's a nickname. His character name, just below it, is written as *Shayna*.

"So, your character is female?" I ask him. I realize Hero conveniently forgot to give his pronouns, like everyone else at the table. It's not the end of the world, I guess, but it's got me a little uneasy.

"Oh, she's *very* female." Hero gives me a broad wink. "Eighteen charisma. I brought a picture, if anyone wants to see it."

Luke glances over with a raised eyebrow. "Sure," he says. "Let's see it."

Hero pulls out a color print-out that looks like it came out of a hentai anime. The woman is so busty, she looks like a chiropractor's nightmare. All of the necessary bits are barely covered with strategic bits of gauzy material.

*Oh, hell.*

Luke's other eyebrow slowly inches up to join the first one. He's radiating such an obviously unimpressed attitude that I'm shocked Hero doesn't just die of embarrassment. "Right," he drawls. "Okay. I think we've all gotten the picture."

Hero rolls his eyes, but doesn't say anything. He tucks the picture next to his character, where he can admire it at his leisure.

Luke exchanges a brief shake of his head with Ginny. I'm still trying to figure out what to do—whether I *should* do anything—when Ginny clears her throat and moves on as though nothing has happened. "So," she says. "Where are we starting?"

I shoot one last uncertain look at Hero, before I take her cue and move on. "Right. Well, you've all been called to the village of Gimlet. The local baron gathers you into his banquet hall to discuss his concerns. There are rumors of undead stirring in the town..."

The opening informational encounter goes off more or less as-intended. I'm a little off-kilter from that weirdness with Hero, but I manage to reclaim my rhythm halfway through. Luke's swashbuckler tries to get the baron to pay him up-front. Ginny's druid unexpectedly takes Luke's side. "I don't trust humans," she declares. "You're all greedy oath-breakers. I will have this money up front, or I will be leaving."

"Oh, sweetheart," Hero sighs, in an overly-affected feminine tone. "You have such an ugly heart for someone so pretty."

Ginny gives him a weird look at being called *sweetheart*. But it's kind of... more or less... in character for his religion, so we all let it pass.

"Oh?" Luke asks archly. "And what about me? Do I have an ugly heart as well—or am I just not pretty?"

Hero waves a hand at Luke. "I expect that sort of thing from a mercenary," he replies. He's clearly uninterested in starting up an exchange with Luke, even with the little roleplaying hook he's been offered.

I clear my throat again. It's getting to be a habit at this table. "Uh... either Luke or Ginny is going to need to roll diplomacy to get your money up front," I say. "One of you can support the other if you like, but I'll need a primary roller."

They chat between them in a low voice, before Luke nods at me. "I've got the higher charisma," he says. "I'll make the roll."

The resulting roll is... underwhelming. But I can feel a little tension at the table, and I don't want to complicate things too much. I let it slide. "You've convinced the baron to pay you up front," I tell them. "He's not happy about it, but he doesn't have many other options at the moment."

The group continues into the adventure proper,

heading out into the cemetery to look for clues. They quickly end up in a fight with a handful of zombies there. Hero knows his abilities, at least—he makes quick work of the undead with a positive channel. Their warlock does a bit of arcane investigation and discovers a ritual spot. It doesn't take them much longer to track down the rich, handsome stranger who arrived in the village only a few months prior.

"Let me do the talking," Hero assures the group. "I'll have him eating out of the palm of my hand."

I have another alarm bell going off in my head. I really don't like where this is heading. Hero winks at me and taps his sheet. "I'm specialized in enchantment," he says. "And since my god is Luin, I have access to the *Charm* spell. I prepare my spell and knock on his door. *Hey, big boy. I heard you ordered a stripper gram!*"

Luke raises his eyes to the ceiling, as though to pray for divine intervention. Ginny is staring down at her sheet, clearly uncomfortable.

*This is my job.* A horrible guilt assaults me. No one at the table wants to say anything, I realize, because it's *my job* to say something.

God, I don't want to say something. The idea is terrifying. But if I'm feeling uncomfortable, I can't *imagine* how Ginny is feeling. I know I can't live with myself if she walks away from this table having *this* as her very first gaming experience.

"Okay," I say slowly. "I'm going to pause things here. Hero—I need to talk to you, please."

Hero grins. "Ooh," he says. "Do I get a *private* scene?"

"No," I say. I'm really trying to keep my voice firm, but it's shaking a little, and I hate that. This guy is taller than me, and older, and I really don't like the way he's looking me up and down right now. "Come on. We're going to step aside for a second."

I get to my feet. Hero frowns and follows suit. We only have to go a table or two away to go unheard—it's so loud in here, the noise quickly drowns everything out. "The character is society-legal," Hero tells me quickly, as I come to a stop. "I checked. All of the abilities stack properly."

"I'm not worried about your *abilities*," I tell him. "I don't know if you've noticed, but you're making the whole table incredibly uncomfortable. I've been trying to let it slide, but I think I probably should have talked to you from the beginning."

Hero scoffs. "What?" he asks. "You mean swash-buckler boy? He's had it out for me *all* game. I didn't even do anything to him."

I massage at my temples. I'm starting to get a headache. "The *whole table*, Hero," I tell him. "Your character is a caricature. The picture was hugely inappropriate. I can't believe I even have to say this, but you *definitely* can't charm an NPC and imply you're there to sex him up."

Hero groans. "Oh my *god*," he says. "I can't believe you're making a big deal out of this. It was a *joke*. Did I seriously hurt your feelings so bad that you have to take me into a corner and give me a lecture?"

I seriously don't know what to do about this. I've got *nothing*. I'm supposed to be in charge, but this guy is looking at me like I'm some teenager whining to him about how the world just isn't fair, instead of a gamemaster discussing sexual harassment with him.

"I'm going to have to ask you to leave the game," I tell him. It's the only thing I can think of to say at this point. It's so incredibly clear that he feels zero shame about his behavior.

"You *what?*" Hero sounds incredulous now. There's a hint of real anger in his tone, and it takes me aback. "Jesus Christ, who hired you to run a game, lady? I have *never* had such a whiny, over-sensitive GM before."

"Oh, I can answer that question for you," Finn says, from behind me. There's an icy chill in his voice that I've never heard before. "I hired her. Actually, I asked her to *volunteer*, as a personal favor to me, and she did. No one here is paid to run games, Mister..." His eyes glance down at the badge. "*Hero.*" The sardonic tone in his voice makes it clear just what he thinks of *that* nickname.

I glance back toward Finn, and I'm ashamed to say my legs are shaking with relief. I've been trying so hard to keep things professional, but deep down, I kind of want to go hide in a bathroom and cry.

Hero is suddenly floundering, now that we have company. He was pretty quick on the draw with insults when it was just me, but now he's clearly searching for the right approach. "Uh," he says slowly. "We were just working out a minor disagreement. I don't think we need another referee over here."

"That's funny," Finn says. He's taken a few steps forward and nudged me subtly behind him. "Because one of the players from your table came to get me specifically. He said you were making an ass of yourself, and that it looked like you were bullying your GM."

*Luke.* I breathe a silent sigh of relief. I'm sure it was him, even if Finn has been careful not to name names.

"We're all here to have fun," Finn informs Hero. "Even the GMs. None of us *have* to be here, getting up at six in the morning and giving up our weekend to run games for you. So if you play the game in a way that ruins other people's fun, you shouldn't be surprised when you get asked to leave."

Hero glances down at Finn's badge. His mouth twists into a scowl. "I didn't realize you were such a white knight, Mister O'Roarke," he observes bitterly. "Oh well. I didn't read your shit anyway."

"You probably should have," Finn tells him shortly. "There's a whole chapter on how to be a considerate player. But since you clearly skipped that homework, I'm putting in a ban on your player account for the next year—including next year's TowerCon." He shakes his head in disgust. "After that, if you want to come back, you'll be on probation until you can prove you know how to act like an adult."

Hero's eyes widen with fury. "Well, I'm pretty sure I *won't* be coming back, if this is what *Towers & Tyrants* has turned into," he spits. "God, you people have *pussified* this game!"

His voice has raised so loudly that even people the next table over can hear him. He turns to kick a chair out from under an empty table. The *clang* startles several players, who look at him with wide eyes.

"Right," Finn says. "That's a lifetime ban. And a call to security." He nods toward one of the beefier volunteers at the door, who's been watching the whole thing with wary interest. The man heads over and grabs Hero by the arm, hauling him bodily for the table, where he orders him to grab his stuff and get out.

Hero is protesting loudly... but that's about *all* he's doing. I wince as I see the whole room following this drama with unabashed interest. But Finn closes an arm around my shoulder, and he leads me away before Hero even reaches the door.

8

## FINN

*I*'m so damned angry I'm still shaking. But Liv is shaking worse. She looks like a kicked puppy. I want to go after that stupid, smug bastard and punch his lights out... but I know security has him in hand, and I *know* that won't make things any better for Olivia.

Instead, I pull her behind the platform where we make announcements, so the curtain shields us from view. Technically, anyone could still walk around the back and see us, but I want to trust people will give us just an inch of privacy, since we so clearly need it.

There's no great place to sit back here. If I'd been thinking, I would've brought a chair. But I don't want to leave Olivia alone, so I sit down on the floor instead and help her down next to me, leaning my back against the platform. I can see tears threatening in her eyes already. I drag her into my arms and hold her tightly.

"I am... *so* sorry," I whisper. "This is all my fault."

She gives a tiny hiccup against my chest, and my

heart breaks. I hate that Liv is sitting here under these too-bright ballroom lights, crying into my shirt. I hate the awful, self-entitled asshole that made her feel like this, when she was doing her best to make sure everyone had a good time.

"It's... n-not your fault," Olivia manages. "It's *my* fault. I let him keep going for so long. My group probably h-hates me."

I groan and tighten my grip on her. "Liv," I say. "None of this is your fault, okay? This is the second game you've ever run. I know five-year veterans who wouldn't know how to deal with a guy like that. You *said* something, and that's way more than most people have the courage to do." I tilt her chin up toward me. Her eyes are already red and puffy. I force a hollow smile. "Hey. How about we just agree that everything is *his* fault and call it a day?"

Liv's lower lip wobbles. She nods, but I can see she's unconvinced.

"I... I left my table alone," Olivia says in a small voice. "I need to go talk to them."

I shake my head. "You don't need to talk to anyone right now," I tell her. "Give me a second." I grab my walkie-talkie from where I left it on the floor next to us. "Can someone please have a quick chat with table four?" I ask. "Tell them their GM is still dealing with a problem. Get them some water bottles, and ask if they need to talk to someone. I'd like to talk to them in a bit too, if I can, but I understand if they don't want to stick around."

*"Roger that,"* says Eric, our volunteer logistics guy. *"Nice volcano just now. I just thought you'd want to know, con management is kicking him out too. They called a cop to give*

*him a talking-to. He's currently shitting his pants in the parking lot."*

Olivia clearly doesn't catch the whole thing, so I relay it to her in slightly less colorful language. She nods tiredly.

"You have a table to run too," she mumbles.

"And I'm sure they're all *very* pissed off at the guy who interrupted their game by having a hissy fit," I say wryly. "If you really don't want me here, Liv, I can go. But if you're just feeling guilty for some reason, then stop. You're upset, and you have every right to be. And I want to hold you and tell you everything's okay—so I'm going to do that now."

Olivia sighs in resignation and relaxes into my arms. I tuck her head beneath my chin and stroke her hair reassuringly.

I don't know how long I actually hold onto Olivia, while she calms down. My back hurts like hell, but I don't want to move until she stops shaking. Eventually, Liv takes a deep breath and looks up at me. Her eyes are dry, if bloodshot. She's put a little steel back into her spine.

"Thank you," Liv says quietly. "For all of that."

I lean down to kiss her gently. It feels like the thing to do, and I'm not interested in asking why. "*All of that* is my responsibility," I tell her. "I would have done... *most* of that... for any gamemaster in this room."

Olivia manages a shaky smile at that. "I was about to say," she mumbles. "The whole kissing-people-on-the-lips thing is very European of you."

"I grew up in Arizona," I tell her, with a deadpan expression. "Anyway—how are you doing?"

Olivia starts pushing to her feet. I get up with her and

help her up, wincing as the blood returns to my legs. "I think I'm okay," she says quietly. "I do want to see if my group is still here, though."

I nod. "Why don't you go clean up in the bathroom and get some water first?" I say. "I'll get some of the official stuff out of the way while you're in there."

It's hard, letting Olivia disentangle herself from me. I want to spend the rest of the day with her, making sure she's okay. But I have a few responsibilities to get out of the way first.

Thankfully, Liv's group *hasn't* left just yet. I notice concerned expressions around the table as I approach, and I know her players have stuck around because they're worried about *her*.

"Hey guys," I say, in the most conciliatory tone I can manage. "I am *so* sorry about your game. I just wanted to let you know that the player in question has been permanently banned from society, and from the convention too. I know that doesn't make up for what you've already experienced, but it's the least that we can do."

Luke, the player who came to get me, rubs his hand over his chin. "Yeah, shit happens, man," he agrees. "I get it. Is Elsinore okay?" He pauses, and glances at Liv's placard again. "Er, *Olivia*," Luke corrects himself. "Sorry, I'm forever gonna have that character name stuck in my head."

"She's... holding up," I say diplomatically. "I asked her to go take a second to breathe. I know she's going to come back and apologize, so I hope you guys will be a little gentle on her. This weekend was her first time GMing, and I kind of pushed her into it at the last second."

Luke whistles to himself, in a kind of *impressed-at-this-*

*disaster* tone. "That is *rough*," he says. "Are we rounding up a posse? Does Mister Hero need a beatdown in the parking lot? Cause I'm up for it if you are."

I wince, but only because that sounds like a *great* plan to my furious, adrenaline-soaked brain. "No, that's not gonna be necessary," I say. "Though I appreciate the thought. *Hero* has been talked to by both security and the police. They're keeping an eye out for him at the door. If he returns to the premises, he'll be arrested for trespassing."

There's a woman sitting next to Luke, doing her best to make herself look as small as possible. The name placard in front of her says her name is Ginny. Now I know why Olivia looked so positively wretched—Ginny looks like she'd rather be just about anywhere else right now. Thankfully, Luke seems to have a friendship of sorts going with her—he's pulled out some playing cards in the interim, and I can see that they've been playing *Go Fish*.

I clear my throat. "Given that you've had your game interrupted," I observe. "I think it's only fair to offer you a new one. I'm booked for most of the convention, but I'd be happy to run you through a different scenario after closing tonight, in the main hotel lobby."

Luke quirks an eyebrow at that. "Much as I appreciate the unexpected lottery win," he says, "I think I'd rather let Olivia give it another whirl. If she's all right with that, of course."

"If I'm okay with what?" Olivia returns just in time to hear the tail-end of the conversation. She's done an admirable job rinsing up; her hair is back in a ponytail again, and the only evidence of her crying is the redness of her eyes.

"I was just telling Mister O'Roarke here that it's a shame I didn't get the chance to properly enjoy your GMing skills," Luke says. "I was wondering if you'd mind running again."

Olivia looks at Luke as though he's grown another head. "You *want* to play in one of my games again?" she asks incredulously.

"Desperately," Luke says, with a deadpan expression. "I'm always going to wonder how it would have gone, otherwise." There's a few other murmurs of encouraging agreement at the table.

I mentally promise myself to give Luke a very nice, personal thank you after all of this is over.

Olivia flushes. "I... I guess I can do that, if you really want," she says. "I understand if no one else wants to play, though." She turns to the rest of the table, and I see the way her eyes keep glancing over toward the woman at the edge. "I am *so* sorry, you guys. I absolutely should have said something from the very beginning. I wish that I had, but I didn't. If anything like this ever happens again, I know I'm going to speak up sooner next time."

Ginny forces a smile. "That didn't look super fun for you either," she says. "I appreciate that you tried to sort it out."

It's a lukewarm reassurance, and I can feel it hit like a dead weight. Olivia looks down at the ground. "Yeah," she mumbles. "Thanks." It's more of an acknowledgement of the situation than a real *thank you.*

Ugh. This is going to hang on Liv for the rest of the con, I *know* it.

"Let me get you guys my number," I say. "Please let me know if you want to follow up any further. In the meantime, we'll have a game waiting for you in the hotel lobby tonight at seven, if you want to join us."

The group sticks around for just a bit longer, working off the remaining tension with a bit of conversation. Eventually though, they begin to dissipate. I nod toward Luke as he heads off and tap at my phone meaningfully. *Call me later,* I imply. He nods back, and strolls off with Ginny.

"Hey," I say to Olivia. "I can cancel my games. I still need to be here to keep an eye on things, but we can just sit and talk for a bit, if you want."

Olivia shakes her head at me. "No," she says. I can hear the disappointment in her voice, but she's slowly getting her strength back all the same. "It's really okay. I've got to meet Emily soon. We've got plans." She forces a smile at me. "Please have *some* fun. I promise I'll be back in a bit."

I sigh and stuff my hands into my pockets. I don't *want* to let her go. Some part of me wants to keep talking through the situation, trying fruitlessly to make it better than it is. But Emily can comfort Olivia just about as well as I can—if not better, in this particular situation—so I nod and let her go.


## OLIVIA

I'm feeling a little less like a total mess, now that I've gotten the chance to wash my face and take a breath. By the time I head out into the hall outside the ballroom, I've gotten back some fragile sense of stability.

It all gets pulled out from under my feet again as I catch sight of Luke and Ginny, talking in a corner of the hallway. Luke has his hand on Ginny's shoulder; she's got her arms crossed over her chest, and she looks far more obviously upset now that she's not in the ballroom with everyone looking at her. I can tell Luke is doing his best to help her calm down, but the sight of that obvious distress on her face just breaks everything open all over again.

I should probably leave it alone. I've already apologized, she's already said it's okay. But I can feel the misery spilling over again, and I'm walking over toward them both, instead of heading for Emily's hotel room, like I should be doing.

Luke sees me first. He keeps a good poker face, but I can see the hint of uncertainty beneath it. Ginny glances up and sees me, and her face freezes.

"I'm sorry." The words are out again before I can stop them. "I'm so sorry. I know I've already said that, but... I'm sorry for *other* things." I draw in a deep, shaky breath. "I was you, like two years ago. And I had... I had *such* a fantastic first GM. Everyone really went out of their way to make me feel welcome. And because of that, I've had... basically, the last two years of my life have been the best *ever*."

I can feel my eyes getting wet again. "I wish I'd been able to do the same for you. And I know you might never want to try another tabletop again, and I don't blame you for that. But I hope you eventually *do* get up the courage, because I want you to have what I have. And if you do, I promise I'll do everything I can to make sure you have the nicest, safest group possible to play with."

Ginny blinks at me. She still looks upset—but there's a funny look on her face now, like she's not sure whether to laugh or cry.

She settles for throwing her arms around me and sniffling into my shirt.

I blink. It's not at all the reaction I was expecting. Ginny is just a little bit smaller than I am—which is saying something—but she gives me the nicest, tightest hug.

"I didn't mean to make you feel bad," Ginny whimpers. "I'm just kind of shellshocked. And... and you have no idea how much that means to me. Just... all of that." She must realize that she's kind of ambushed me with the hug, because she tries to pull back in embarrassment—but I hold on tighter and breathe a sigh of relief.

*This is okay,* I think tiredly. *We're both eventually going to be okay.*

It doesn't dispel my misery completely, but it wipes away a big portion of it. I know I'll feel better about this in just a few days, instead of flashing back to it at random intervals from now until forever, wondering if I'm some kind of horrible person for screwing up so badly.

Ginny gives me a watery smile. "It was kind of scary," she admits, in a softer tone. She doesn't look at Luke as she says it. I have a feeling that *scary* is not a word she's used to describe things to him so far. No matter how nice he is, Luke is still a guy with a decent bit of muscle on him, and there's no way he'll ever fully understand what it's like to be a small woman with a tall, angry man throwing a temper tantrum nearby. There's a kind of comfort in sharing that fear with another woman who *gets* it.

Ginny takes another breath, still holding onto me. "I'm playing board games with Luke for the next little bit," she says. "And... I'm going to come to the game tonight. I'm not gonna lie, it's got me a little intimidated. But I know you did a hard thing because I was uncomfortable. So I think it's only fair that I do something hard for you too." Her shaky smile crinkles a little wider. "It's good to know I have a few people that'll have my back."

"Elsie's a paladin," Luke tells Ginny. "So she'll have your front. I enjoy dirty backstabbing tricks, so *I'll* watch your back." He turns his attention back to me as he leans back against the wall, stuffing his hands in his pockets. "We're about to go collect sheep and rocks on a hex map for a bit. You want to join us?"

I bite my lower lip, as Ginny and I slowly let go of each other. "I'd really love to," I admit. "But I planned something with my roommate months ago, and I really think she might murder me in my sleep if I skip out."

Luke nods sagely. "Good excuse," he says. "Oh well. More sheep for the two of us, I guess."

Ginny steps back and wipes at her face. "I'll see you tonight," she promises me.

The two of them head off for the board game room. I let out a deep, relieved sigh. A whole lot of stress goes with it.

It's a good thing Emily is so good with makeup. Between last night and everything that's happened today already, I'm pretty sure what's left of my eyeliner has turned me into a racoon.

9

## OLIVIA

Emily is waiting for me in the hotel room she booked just for this purpose. Samson and Jim are already there—they've gotten through some of their own preparations without me. True to form, Emily is still wearing just her little silk dressing gown, with her makeup half-done; she's been so focused on helping everyone else that she hasn't even gotten around to finishing her foundation yet. With just her base coating and no contouring, she looks a little bit like a ghost.

"Liv!" she calls out, as I head through the door. "Thank god, what took you so long? I was starting to worry—*oh!*" Emily's eyes widen as she catches sight of my puffy eyes and smeared eyeliner. "Ohmygosh, what happened?"

Samson peers over Emily's shoulder at me. He's wearing a full chain shirt, but it might as well be made of feathers for all that it weighs him down. The linen tabard that hangs over it is *fantastic*—it's tastefully ragged, slashed through in strategic places to make it look like it's been through a few battles. I know then that Emily must have stolen the tabard from Samson for a few touch-ups, even though she swore she wouldn't have time to work on anyone else's stuff in the last month leading up to the con.

Jim is utterly resplendent in the awful, violet-striped tights that we all decided his bard wears. *Medieval fashion disaster* doesn't begin to cover it, with his overly-feathered cap and his multicolored bracers of armor. But the true masterpiece is—my *god*—the absolutely genuine lute he's strapped across his back.

I find myself staring in mute amazement for a good few seconds before I'm able to speak. "*Wow*," I manage finally. "Holy hell." A giggle escapes me, in spite of the rough morning I've had. "Our party is *real*."

Emily smiles proudly at that. As well she should—I might have come up with the idea, but Emily is the one who really took off running with it. She's a semi-professional cosplayer, and she's good enough at it that she's got her own tiny cult following online. I know she's been carefully documenting the whole process of our group's transformation so she can post blogs and videos about it later, once the surprise is sprung.

"You look like you just got a face-full of pepper spray," Samson tells me dubiously.

I wince at the reminder. "Yeah," I mumble. "It's been… a morning. I'll fill you guys in while I get dressed."

I do just that, as Emily helps me into my own costume. I leave out the more, er, personal parts between me and Finn. I'm not quite sure I'm ready to share those with Emily. I'm still feeling wrung out, and not nearly as happy as I should be about the kind of epic night I just had. I want to be in a better mood when I tell Emily about it, so I can savor the conversation.

"I'm sorry we weren't there," Jim sighs. "No one ever says stupid shit like that when Samson is around. He's like a magical ward against douchebags."

Samson snorts. "There's nothing magical about it," he says. "I spend most of my life in the gym. I don't even have to try and look scary for people to act like I'm gonna break them in two." Samson works as a personal trainer. I don't actually like the idea of using him as some kind of big man-shield, but he's assured me more than once that he's pleased to serve in that capacity.

"I'm honestly working my way through it," I assure them both. "I just want to focus on our big project now. I'm really dying to see Finn's face when we show up."

Emily helps me into my armor harness as we talk. It's more like an armor half-harness, if I'm going to be honest —she offered to help me make some Warbla plate mail, but it turns out I'm more enthused by the *idea* of plate mail than I am about actually wearing it. I've got a few artful pieces of armor over my gambeson, with the implication that I'm partway through pulling on the rest of my battle gear.

"Okay," Emily gushes. "I think the half-armored look is really doing it for you." She grabs a brush and a hairdryer and teases at a few strands of my hair. At some point, Emily sticks the brush between her teeth, fumbling around for something behind her. Jim sighs and dutifully hands her a can of hairspray, and I get the impression they've been through this routine a dozen times already this morning. I close my eyes just in time for her to spritz whatever finishing touches she needs on my hair.

*"Perrfuct!"* Emily mumbles around the brush. She spits it out into her hand and grabs for one of the *many* makeup palettes she's got lying out on the hotel dresser. "Okay, come on into the light where I can see you better. We're gonna do your base makeup, and *then* we're gonna do that scar over your nose, from when that frost giant smacked you in the face."

I blink quickly. "What about you?" I protest. "You're not even dressed, Em!"

Emily waves a hand dismissively. "I can do myself up in no time, babe. Don't worry about it so much."

I *do* worry about it—but for once, Emily's not exaggerating. The moment she finishes rubbing a dozen different brushes over my face, she's already slipping into a slinky, shimmering gown. Five minutes later, Emily looks like a half-elven femme fatale, with gently pointed ears and thigh-high boots. She tugs on a bodice and crooks a finger at Samson. "*Now* you can be a big, strong man for me," Emily tells him wryly. "Here—tug the laces like this. You're aiming for *hourglass figure.* If you hear a rib crack, you've gone too far."

I've got to admit—only fifteen minutes into her costume, Em is already the sexiest thing at this convention. And I'm counting the con-exclusive, early-release T&T modules they have for sale in the dealer's room in that estimation.

"God damn," I tell her. "You're gonna do area-of-effect damage in that costume. And I *don't* mean with a fireball."

Emily grins breathlessly at me in the mirror as she pats contouring onto her cheekbones. "Alas," she says. "I have no one in particular to slay this time. But I think the channel's going to love it."

Jim strums at his lute idly as she talks. I'm far from a musical expert, but I'm pretty sure the instrument is out of tune. He's still got a broad smile on his face. I wonder where the hell he managed to find the instrument.

"Okay!" Emily quickly packs up her makeup and turns to face us, smoothing down her shimmering peacock dress. "Let's do this thing!" She starts for the door—pauses, then turns on me. "Wait! You're missing something very important, Dame Elsinore!"

I blink. Emily ducks behind the bed and grabs a tall, mirrored shield with a significant crack running down the middle. It's a minor artifact of Luin—a custom item I picked up after a personal holy quest. I grab it from her with a sigh of relief. I spent *forever* on that thing. I can't imagine how upset I'd be if I left it behind at the last second.

"*Now* we're ready!" Emily declares. She hikes up her gorgeous skirt in one hand. "Let's go make Finn O'Roarke lose his ever-loving mind."


## FINN

I'm pretty damned exhausted by the time the ballroom winds down. Thankfully, my last game is done—all I've got left is a bit of supervision while the latest tables tie up loose ends in their games. After a bit of texting back and forth, Luke has headed back from his afternoon of board games to chat with me while I choke down a sandwich and try to catch my breath.

"I swear, I've run for you before," I tell him. We've

perched ourselves on the front of the stage for now, away from the tables where the last games are still running. "You played... a priest?"

"A priest of Berlisle," Luke agrees, leaning against the stage next to me. He's got that same ever-present expression on his face as before—something halfway between blandly indifferent and mildly interested in everything at once. "He's too high-level for most of these tabletops, though. I might dust him off for the next epic event."

"Berlisle," I mumble into my sandwich. "That's right. You know, I wouldn't have pegged you for playing a devil-worshipper."

Luke shoots me a half-smile. "If you're playing a priest of Berlisle *correctly*, then most people wouldn't."

I shake my head. "I really appreciate everything you did today," I tell him. "It's hard to corral a bunch of strangers like this. Every time I think I've got the hang of it, something like this happens, and I remember how much I rely on the other players at the table."

Luke frowns. "I didn't do as much as I should have," he admits. "I fell back into the T&T mindset a little bit—didn't pause the game and check in with everyone. Honestly, if I'd been thinking more, I would have spoken up from the get-go and saved Elsie all that trouble."

I blink at him. It takes me a second to realize Luke is talking about Olivia. He must have forgotten her real name again. "Her name's Olivia," I remind him helpfully. "Though I'm sure she'd still respond to Elsinore."

Luke waves a hand. "Elsie," he mutters. "I'm not breaking the habit *now*, so I might as well go with it."

I consider him curiously. "What do you mean exactly, by... the *T&T mindset?*"

Luke blinks. For the first time, he looks a little abashed. "Er, sorry," he says, with a hint of sheepishness. "That must have sounded a little derisive. I don't mean to be insulting, but T&T has always been a little... *lacking*, in out-of-character regulation. It's been catching up a bit lately, but it's still got a long way to go. I dabble in Nordic LARP when I'm not here. It's all... consent-based rules, active checking in with each other to make sure no one's upset." He pauses, and coughs. "I'm into, uh... *dark* Nordic LARP. The kind you really need those rules for, in my opinion. But a few of those concepts might not go amiss in Tower Society, if you wanted to incorporate them."

Luke is clearly doing his best to step gently around the subject. My initial instinct is to get defensive—I'm a well-known, respected game writer in the industry, for all that I make my living at something else. I've been running whole rooms full of tabletops for at least a decade now, and this is the first really major incident I've ever had. Hell, people enter into lotteries just to sit at my table: I must be doing *something* right. But I stop the knee-jerk response and chew on it a bit.

I never thought of myself as the sort to get arrogant. But now that I examine myself a little more closely, I realize I've started taking for granted that there's nothing new anyone can teach me about gaming. That's a dangerous attitude to have, for someone who runs major con events. I've got the opportunity for a different perspective here—a perspective that might have prevented what happened today. One that *might* prevent it from happening again, if I'm lucky.

"Thanks," I say finally. "I think I'd like to have a

longer chat with you about that. I don't guess you're local?"

"I am, actually," Luke says. "Or... more or less. I'm out in Plano."

"Huh," I mutter. "I'm in Richardson. We'll have to sit down to dinner sometime soon."

I'm already trying to schedule something out in my head, juggling my work and my game sessions around to find an opening. It's maybe understandable then that I don't immediately recognize the group of cosplayers that have walked into the ballroom.

"Oh hey, Finn," Eric says to me, as he heads over to gently interrupt our conversation. "Sorry to bug you guys —I've just got to grab you for something real quick. It's kind of important."

Ergh. God, I hope it's not another emergency. I've only barely made it to the end of Sunday, and I'm pretty much out of organizer juice at this point. "Yeah?" I ask him, turning around. "What's the problem?"

Eric is grinning at me in a way that suggests he's in on some secret I don't know about. I knit my brow. He grabs me cheerfully by the arm and nudges me around to face the group that's just headed up toward the stage.

My mouth drops.

It's not just any cosplayers. It's *my group*. All four of them are here, dressed as their characters from my game. And holy hell, the *detail*. I'm not even sure where to rest my eyes first. Samson has his actual holy symbol on his tabard, straight from the illustration the artist did for the *Divine Compendium*. Jim is wearing those *hideous* violet-striped tights—I never imagined he was the sort of guy to volunteer himself to look so silly. Emily is so picture-perfect as her fashionista transmuter that she ought to be Miss July in some T&T calendar. She's even got the opal necklace her character stole off Keller in our third session.

My eyes finally come to rest on Olivia. And I'm pretty sure I actually blue-screen for a second.

Dame Elsinore is standing right in front of me, wearing a shy grin. Her cheeks are pink, but her posture is straighter and more confident than I'm used to seeing from Liv. She looks like an honest-to-god medieval knight; there's a quilted coat bound around her waist with a leather belt, and a few pieces of plate armor strapped to a chest harness. They're so realistic that I have to look twice to realize they're *not* made of real metal, but some cosplay material I've seen Emily use before in her stuff.

She's wearing all white and gold—Luin's colors. And there's a mirrored shield with a single crack running down the middle, strapped to her arm. I *know* I'm staring at her like I've gone crazy.

I have to fight the sudden, irrational urge to go sweep her up in my arms and kiss her, right in the middle of the ballroom. Actually... I'm not fighting it very hard at all. I've already taken a single step toward her when I hear Emily's voice, and stop partway.

"And *that*, folks and artichokes, is Finn O'Roarke, getting his first look at his real-life T&T group." Emily has pulled out her phone to film my reaction. There's a deep-seated glee in her tone as she speaks to the mic.

I stare at Liv... but force myself back. *Later,* I think. I'm going to... *do things* to her. Later. After I'm done thanking my group, and helping run an extra game in a hotel lobby, and I've got the chance to drive her back to my place.

Olivia meets my eyes and instantly flushes. I wonder if she knows what I'm thinking. If she does, she's definitely not being specific enough or dirty enough.

"So?" Emily prompts me. "Any further comments for the audience, Mister O'Roarke?"

"Holy mother of god," I breathe. A hundred weird little things from the last few months click into place at once. I turn on Jim, incredulous. "You asked me for the 3D printer files for your figurines. You said you just wanted to buy the hardware and test it out. That was back in *January*."

Jim nods reasonably, as though we're discussing a server update at work. "I mean, yes," he says. "You'd have immediately suspected something if *Emily* asked for the files."

"This is... *nuts*." I can't stop shaking my head. "Oh my god." I know I've got an absolutely insane smile spreading across my face. "You guys look *amazing*. I can't imagine the amount of work this must have taken."

I want to give them all the attention and gratitude they deserve, but I literally can't find words good enough for the task. Just as I'm stringing together something halfway decent in my head, Jim pulls an actual, honest-to-god *lute* from off his back, and strums the strings discordantly.

"You... you got a fucking *lute*," I manage.

Samson shoots me a long-suffering look. "He got a fucking lute," he says.

Jim grins. "I tried to learn *Hot Cross Buns*, but it's

apparently beyond my musical skills. Maybe I should have gone with the tuba."

"Wait, wait, wait," Emily interrupts enthusiastically. She hands her phone to Samson, so he can keep filming. "We're not done *yet*." She clips over toward me, shoving a tall bag into my hands. "Open it up!"

I dig into the bag, almost on autopilot. I can't stop sneaking awed looks at the group in front of me. But my hands grasp leather, and I pull out what looks to be…

…a very ragged leather hat.

Just like the one on Keller's figurine.

Emily plucks the hat from my hands and settles it atop my head. "Would you care to join us for a picture, Your Highness?" she asks archly.

I laugh. This is… *amazing*. Now I *really* have no words.

Samson hands the phone off to Eric, who's clearly been in on this the whole time. My group settles in around me, mugging for the camera. Emily shoves Olivia bodily at me, and I catch her just in time, blinking.

"What are you *waiting* for, you moron?" Emily asks me in exasperation. There's a haughty look on her unnaturally narrow-looking face. I have no idea how she managed those elven features with just makeup. "I swear, I have been an *exemplary* wingman for you for the last two years," Emily tells me. "But I've got twenty bucks to win, and if you don't kiss this woman right now, I'm going to start digging around the ballroom to make sure she goes home with *someone* who appreciates this costume."

I blink. I'm suddenly incredibly glad I've gotten some practice in for this by now, because I can't imagine how dumbfounded I'd be feeling otherwise. I look down at

Liv, who's currently doing her best impression of a tomato.

There's an adorable little scar across the very top of her nose. It should not turn me on nearly as much as it does. But Emily is right—I definitely need to kiss this woman.

"Do you mind?" I mumble at her.

Olivia wraps her arms shyly around my neck in reply. "Please do," she says softly.

I sweep her into a dramatic dip for the camera—and press my lips against hers. She lets out a gasp against me, tightening her fingers behind my neck. Her lips don't taste like strawberries anymore. They're some sugar-vanilla flavor instead—whatever lipstick Emily has picked out for her character. I run my tongue over the edge of her bottom lip, savoring the sweetness. She angles her neck to deepen the kiss, and I'm so dizzy with the feel of her in my arms that I can barely hear the din of applause that's kicked up around the room. Realistically, none of the players here know what the hell is going on. But everyone loves a good show, and my group has put on a pretty fantastic display.

Emily crows in victory. The sound washes over me, but somehow it's not quite loud enough to drown out Liv's soft breath, or the tiny, almost indistinct moan she makes against my mouth.

I catch my breath, staring down into those soft hazel eyes.

"I told you I'd sweep you off your feet, Sparrow," I whisper.

Olivia smiles up at me in pure delight. "Only because

I *let* you do it," she murmurs back to me, with a hint of sass.

The pictures continue in quick succession. Emily insists on getting everyone in all kinds of different poses—she even makes Jim get down on one knee to pretend to serenade his husband with the lute. It's the first time I've ever seen Samson blush in public, and I'm glad we've got a photo for posterity.

In between pictures, I become dimly aware of Luke, standing off to one side. I'd nearly forgotten he was with me when the craziness began. But that blasé expression of his has cracked just a little bit—he keeps blinking at Emily as though he's been hit by a truck. On the one hand, I can't really blame him—if I wasn't still holding the most adorable paladin in the world in my arms, I might have to admit that Emily looks like something between a glamorous movie elf and a sexy Bond girl. But I don't think that's *all* that has him staring. He's just a little too floored for that.

"God damn," Luke manages, as he catches my eyes. He shakes his head incredulously. "You run a game for *Silverhart?* You lucky bastard, you."

Oh. *Ohh.* I grin dazedly. Silverhart is Emily's online handle for her cosplaying channel. "I am indeed a lucky bastard," I admit. But I'm mostly looking at Liv as I say it. She's wiggled her way underneath my arm, and I know I'm going to have a hard time letting her go.

"Em really did a ton of the work," Olivia admits. There's a breathless, almost frantic tone to her voice. "I kept telling her not to stress over it, and she swore she was just going to give the rest of us advice, but all the really cool stuff was hers—"

"Liv came up with the idea," Emily interrupts, in a song-song sort of voice. "She's the one who organized all the sneaking behind your back and worked out our meetings in between games."

Olivia gives a sheepish grin. It's half-pleased, half-mortified. "I... I tried to do my part," she says.

I shake my head at her in amazement. I don't think anyone's ever done something this fantastic for me before, *ever*. "Why?" I ask, perplexed. "I mean... it's nowhere near my birthday. Christmas is months away. Is there some special occasion I'm missing?"

Olivia smiles softly at me. There's a hint of nostalgia on her face. "Well... *yeah*," she says. "I played my very first T&T game two years ago." She takes my hand, threading her fingers into mine. "I've really... really enjoyed myself since then. Mostly because of all the work you put into our game. And I wanted... we *all* wanted to thank you for that."

If you had asked me just an hour earlier what I thought of tabletop gaming, I might have given you a bit of a depressing answer. Given all the stress and responsibility and misery I've been under for the last little bit, I might have said some less than flattering things about my passion of choice for the last decade and change.

But this crazy, implausible, *transcendent* feeling I've got in my chest right now reminds me of the very first game I ever ran. Looking down at Liv, I remember when I first decided I wanted to write a game of my very own.

For the most part, I think, the gamers I've got around me are pretty fucking fantastic people.

And I *love* running games for them.

I look down into Olivia's eyes. "You're right," I say.

"This is a pretty great anniversary." I lean down to press my forehead to hers. "I'm really glad I met you, Liv," I whisper to her.

Liv blinks back tears—but I don't think I've ever seen her look so blissfully happy. "I'm really glad I met you too," she whispers back.

# EPILOGUE
## OLIVIA

**SIX MONTHS LATER.**

"There's a lot of work ahead of you in the years to come," Finn informs our group, as we huddle around the coffee table. "But for now, you've liberated your country and re-installed Princess Ephram on the throne. Sorry—*Queen* Ephram now, I suppose." He leans back in his chair with a pleased expression. "She sets out a banquet in your honor. It's the biggest event of the year—you can see a number of familiar faces mingling in the crowd."

"Ooh, in *that* case," Emily says, sitting upright. "Julianna is wearing a *very* special dress for the occasion. Just assume she took twenty on her Craft: Tailor roll."

Finn spreads his hands accommodatingly. "Tell me about this magnificent dress," he insists. "This is the last session, so it's the last dress you get to make with this character. It's got to be pretty over-the-top."

Emily chews at her lip, glancing sideways at me. "Ugh, last dress," she mutters. "I'm not emotionally prepared for this, Liv. What do I do?"

I blink. "You're the fashionista wizard," I protest, "not me."

Emily sighs. "Um. Okay. I guess... oh!" She snaps her fingers. "I still have that extra set of Heavenly Armor we never used. I cannibalize it for materials and turn it into a celestial gown. Gauzy stuff, white and silver, big angelic wings on the back—the full works."

Samson snorts. "Julianna is the *last* person who should be wearing angelic raiment," he observes wryly.

Emily grins at him. "That's why it's a *costume*, Samson," she says. "I'm dressing up as something I'm not."

"Your dress is naturally the talk of the whole city," Finn assures her. "In fact, you manage to start up rumors that some angel has blessed Queen Ephram's reign."

Emily beams, scribbling a little note to herself in her game journal for posterity. I'm almost positive she'll be working on a concept sketch of her latest celestial design as soon as she gets home tonight.

"I've got the music covered," Jim tells us. He strums idly at the real lute sitting in his lap. "Anyone who asks for *Free Bird* is getting a tuba to the face, though."

"Funny you should say that," Samson deadpans. "I've got a song request—"

"Don't you start," Jim groans.

"Queen Ephram intercepts Llew just before he can make it to his husband," Finn informs Samson. "She asks if you've considered her request any further. She's going to have to pick her new religious advisor soon."

Samson frowns. "Uhh... damn," he mutters. "I'm so torn. It's a real opportunity to do some good. But I really don't know if Llew is interested in settling down in one place for so long."

Jim strums the lute again, raising his eyebrows. "I'm going to be running the bardic college here," he says. "You'd best find *something* that keeps you in the city. Unless you're not interested in supporting my music career?"

Samson rubs at his chin. "Okay," he acknowledges. "Fair point. Llew will accept the position for *now*. But we're going to need to leave on the occasional adventure, or else he's gonna go stir-crazy."

"Done and done," Jim agrees. "High Priest Llew it is."

"And will Dame Elsinore be accepting the position of Chief Diplomat?" Finn asks me.

I chew on my lip. "Well... it sounds right up Elsinore's alley," I admit. "But it would involve a lot of traveling around, wouldn't it? I'd be away from the city almost all the time. And I've got, um. *Things* here." That's the point that makes me feel a little uncertain. I kind of like the idea of Elsinore getting a happily-ever-after with Keller, but it doesn't sound like that would be an option if she takes a diplomatic position. He's still more-or-less in charge of the thieves' guild, and unlikely to be leaving the city.

"Oh, about that," Finn says casually. He's got that sparkle in his eyes again that tells me he's got a plan. "Someone *else* has shown up to the banquet. You get a tap on your shoulder. *Aren't you going to dance, Sparrow?*"

Emily grabs the bowl of popcorn again, without missing a beat.

I flush as I recognize the voice Finn uses for Keller. "Er... *of course*," I say, in Elsinore's voice. "*I was waiting for the right man to show up and ask.*"

There's a funny feeling in the room that I can't quite put my finger on. Samson's normally the sort to go for his phone when the scene switches away from him, but he's watching with rapt attention. Jim is trying very hard not to look at me for some reason. Emily is shovelling popcorn into her mouth like there's no tomorrow—though that's hardly uncommon.

"*It was awfully nice of everyone to put this party together for me,*" Finn jokes. "*You didn't all have to come out here just for my retirement, but I do appreciate it.*"

"*Retirement?*" I blink a few times. "Wait... you mean Keller isn't in charge of the thieves' guild anymore?"

"He's not," Finn says innocently. "Given his recent change in outlook, running the thieves' guild has been suiting him less and less. In fact, he's offered to act as the personal bodyguard for the queen's new Chief Diplomat. It's a bit of a career change, but perhaps it'll give him a chance to do something *above-board* for a bit."

I grin at that. "That sounds like a good opportunity," I agree. "Maybe the Chief Diplomat can be persuaded to accept him, if he's *very* charming."

"Hm." Finn nods slowly, and I can *feel* everyone else at the table leaning in as he speaks now. "*I hope the Chief Diplomat is amenable to open bribery,*" he says. "*Why don't you check your pocket, little Sparrow?*"

I frown. "Uh... I guess I check my pocket?" I say. "He didn't *steal* something for me, did he?"

Finn's lips twitch upward. "Oh no," he says. "Keller wouldn't dare. He knows how you feel about stolen goods." He holds my eyes with his, and now I *know* something weird is going on. "Why don't you check your jacket pocket, Liv?"

I knit my brow. When I shove my hand into my jacket pocket, I find a small box inside that *definitely* wasn't there when I first settled in for game. My eyes widen, and I shoot an incredulous look at Emily, who's looking *very* smug over her popcorn. She's been sitting just close enough all night that I suspect she slid the box into my pocket while I wasn't paying attention.

It's a tiny, black velvet box.

I press my hand to my mouth. *Oh my god.* No wonder everyone's been weird all night. They all *knew* this was coming.

"You gonna open the box or what?" Emily prompts me impatiently.

My hands shake as I flick it open. There's a delicate silver ring inside, set with a shimmering peacock-like opal. I know in that moment that Finn must have gotten it custom-made, through the same artisan that helped Emily with her opal necklace.

I've got tears in my eyes, and I'm not even embarrassed.

Finn heads over from his chair. He takes the box from me gently and gets down on one knee. He swallows hard, and I can see the nervousness in his brown eyes. "I am very in love with you, Olivia Walker," he tells me. "And I know it's a little soon—but I was hoping that you'd kindly consider spending the rest of your life with me."

I don't trust myself to speak. I nod quickly, with my hand still over my mouth.

Finn slips the ring onto my finger, and Emily lets out

a long, relieved breath. I can't imagine why she thought I might have *ever* said no, but it seems her ultimate ship has finally come to fruition, either way.

I throw my arms around Finn and kiss him harder than I've ever kissed him before.

"This wedding is going to be *so* geeky," Samson mutters to Jim, with obvious approval in his voice. "Do you think we'll get to use our costumes again?"

"I'm doing the bride's makeup!" Emily insists gleefully. "Oh, my god. Liv is going to need a dress, too. What kind of *dress* is she going to wear?"

They start chatting behind me, but I can't make heads or tails of any of it. I was convinced that Finn would never top that session when we took down Roland, but I was totally wrong.

This. *This* is the best game I've ever played.

"I love you so much," I mumble into his mouth, still blinking back tears.

"I love you too," Finn murmurs. "And just think. We've got a *lot* more games ahead of us."

He's absolutely right. And I absolutely can't wait.

THE END

# A WICKED ENCOUNTER

**EMILY**

I've been waiting half a year to play this game, but all I can think about is the hot blond guy leaning back in the chair directly next to me.

It's been six months since our regular gaming group finished its two-year-long campaign. I had to retire Julianna, my half-elven fashionista transmuter. I'm not gonna lie, I had a sniffle in the car afterward.

Okay, the sniffling *might* have had something to do with the fact that our gamemaster Finn used the last session to romantically propose to my roommate Liv... but I was also really emotional about putting the last bookend on that character's story.

Thankfully, my roommate is basically the best. Liv's been stretching her own storytelling muscles in the last year, and she promised the whole group that she'd run something special for us at TowerCon this year—a game where we'd get to bring back our old characters for one last hurrah. Liv even told Finn he could jump in and play Keller, one of his non-player characters from the game.

So here we are, all settled around the table in a hotel lobby on the Saturday night of TowerCon, while Liv sets the scene for the game. Only, there's two more people at the table than I was expecting, and one of them is *painfully* distracting.

"I hope you guys don't mind," Liv says shyly. "I don't see Luke and Ginny very often, and I really wanted to run something for them while I was at the con. I figured they could just guest star, since we're playing tonight anyway?"

There's a chorus of enthusiastic agreement around the table. Finn already knows both Luke and Ginny, and Samson and Jim are some of the most welcoming players I know. I mumble my own *yeah, sure,* sneaking peeks at the two players that have joined the table.

I dimly remember Ginny from last year's convention. She's short and adorable, with rounded cheeks and blonde pixie hair, streaked with pink highlights. Poor Ginny's very first game of *Towers & Tyrants* had a bad player at the table, and I know Liv's been beating herself up for forever because she thinks she didn't handle things well enough as the gamemaster. Ginny seems to have really bounced back from that experience in the last year, though—she's fully enthused for this year's con, dressed up in a green druid's robe and wearing latex elf ears. The costume isn't professional quality, but she's cute as a button, so she really makes it work.

Luke is... not adorable. No, *adorable* is not a word I'd use to describe him. *Sexy,* maybe. *A really good bad idea waiting to happen,* for sure. He's a long, lean specimen of a man, with dirty blond hair that falls into his eyes. *Blue eyes.* I already know that, because I've been looking at him *way* too much. Luke isn't costumed at all—at least, not in the usual way. He's dressed nicely, with a black button-down and slacks and a black-and-gold vest. Liv has already assured me he's the nicest guy in the world, but there's a kind of devil-may-care smirk on his lips that already has me going

I have a thing for bad boys. It's almost like a disease. I blame my mother's copy of the movie *Labyrinth*. Ever since I watched it, I've had confusing feelings for blond, villainous men in formal clothing. Add a little guyliner, and I'm basically instant putty.

Luke isn't wearing guyliner, but he's got the well-dressed bad boy thing down pat. "You're sure you're good with me playing a lawful evil character?" he asks Liv skeptically. He *does* have a friendly voice, for all that he looks wickedly delicious.

"I've already accounted for it!" Liv says cheerily. "You guys will have mutual goals. I believe your cleric's god still hates demons?"

"Oh, he *certainly* does," Luke agrees. "Demons are far too unpredictable. Berlisle prefers his wickedness a little more disciplined."

I can't believe what I'm hearing. We're going to have a cleric of Berlisle in the group? "You're playing a *devil-worshipper?*" I manage.

Luke shoots me a winning smile that makes me go weak in the knees. He reaches out to take my hand and pretends to brush his lips across the back. His breath ghosts over my skin, and I shiver. "Archbishop Devlin Carr," he says. "At your service. I assure you, all of the terrible stories you've heard about me are absolutely true."

Oh. Sweet baby Jesus.

Luke lets go of my hand without another thought, as though he *didn't* just inspire me to imagine those lips traveling up my arm, and on to... other places.

"Ginny will be playing Queen Isadora Ephram," Liv tells us. "I made her up a character sheet. She'll be joining you for your mission undercover. Everyone in the group but Devlin will know who she is, obviously."

Luke shoots Ginny an arched eyebrow. "And who brought *this* useless chickadee?" he jokes.

Ginny rolls her eyes and smacks him on the shoulder. "You be careful, wise-ass," she says. "If you mouth off like that to me in-character, I could have you thrown in a dungeon."

Apart from the unique *distraction* that Luke brings to the table, I'm actually getting a good feeling off these two. They're clearly comfortable enough with each other to add a little edge to their banter.

"Before I forget," our bard Jim notes from my other side, "anyone want a beer? Liv said we're allowed to drink at her game, as long as we accept the natural conse-quences of our *impaired decision-making*." He grins at that.

Our cleric of luck, Samson, grabs a beer from under-neath the table. "I'm gonna need to be *very* drunk, if you're playing that lute during game," he mutters. Jim strums the actual, honest-to-god lute he bought last year for his bard's costume. He has no idea how to play it. It's *also* wildly out of tune. I groan and grab a beer for myself.

"Yes, please," Luke says next to me. His voice is low

and amused. "I never turn down an opportunity to indulge my vices."

I can't help squirming just a little bit at that. I'd love to indulge *his* vices.

Ahem.

I pass a beer over in his direction, and Liv begins setting the scene for us.

## LUKE

God, I wish I was evil sometimes.

Ginny likes to make fun of me; she says I play evil characters so much because I'm secretly lawful good and kind of miserable about it. Frankly, she's not so far off the mark.

Right now, for example. I'm sitting next to the most stunning woman at this convention, wishing I cared less about the game I've been invited to and the feelings of its gamemaster. If I was less of a total sap, maybe I'd be openly hitting on the frankly gorgeous woman next to me, instead of consciously avoiding any hint of impropriety. I've seen what happens when guys corner a female player at the gaming table, and it's just not pretty.

But holy hell, does it *hurt* to be good. Emily is actually dressed up as her character—and I don't mean that in the casual sense. She's a professional cosplayer with her own online channel, which I *might* watch religiously. She's wearing a slim, peacock-colored dress that hugs her curves, slitted *very* high up on her legs to display those thigh-high leather boots of hers. I know for a fact that the bodice she's wearing to force that hourglass shape makes it hard for her to breathe—especially when she's sitting down, like she currently is—because she laughed about it at length in one of her videos. Emily's wearing honest-to-god elf ears, carefully painted to match her own skin tone... but the long red hair that spills down her shoulders is the real deal.

I've got the sexiest geek in the entire state of Texas sitting next to me, and I'm forcing myself not to act like I'm wildly attracted to her.

Evil people do not have this problem, god damn it.

"Elsinore is stalling for time at the negotiating table," Liv tells us, "but she can only do it for so long." Our gamemaster is blissfully unaware of my mental anguish. "You've only got a few hours to figure out which emissary is actually a demon in disguise."

"We'll need to search their rooms," Ginny says imperiously, "starting with *this* room." She turns toward Finn, at the edge of the table. "You—thief. Burglary is your speciality, isn't it? You can open this lock?"

Finn makes a show of sighing heavily. "I don't think anyone has ever so understated my skills before," he says. "Yes. I can unlock a door, Your Ma—" He side-eyes my character and changes his words midstream. "You're *mad* if you think I can't," he corrects himself.

I snort at that. It's an unexpected pleasure getting to play at a table with Finn. I'm a little less star-struck by his presence these days, since we've spent the last year occasionally hanging out over drinks, but he's still a well-loved gamewriter for T&T. Finn happens to have written the *Infernal Villains* sourcebook, which I use... rather a lot.

"Well then," Ginny declares. "There's no time like the present. The Chief Diplomat can't keep those scoundrels busy forever. Archbishop, I presume you'll know signs of demonic rituals if you see them?"

I blink. *Right.* I'm the Archbishop. She's addressing *me.* I haven't gotten to play Devlin in far too long—he's too high-level for most games. "I'm not sure whether I should take that as a compliment or resent the implications," I observe. "But yes. I'm well-learned in the ways of demons... and how best to remove them from this plane of existence."

The other cleric of the group—I think the player's name was Samson—gives me a narrow-eyed gaze. He's built like a tank, so it's a little intimidating *out-of-character* as well. "Don't think I don't have my eye on you, you devilish bootlicker," he tells me.

I throw him my best, most charming smile. "Now, I'm fairly certain *that* was a compliment," I tell him. "It's all right—I'm used to people being wildly attracted to me. You don't need to be embarrassed."

Jim, the bard, reaches out to press a hand against Samson's chest. "*Don't* let the devil-worshipper wind you up," he warns. "You're just entertaining him."

Samson lets out a low growl and crosses his arms.

"Wildly attracted to you?" Emily asks. She wrinkles her nose at me. "In *those* robes? With *that* broach? Oh *lord,* no. You need to reassess your wardrobe, sweetheart."

Oof. I know that's just an in-character zing, but that *stings.* I shake my head in her direction. "I fail to understand why *she's* here," I observe to the group. "Did someone need a dress made?"

Emily's lips twitch with humor, though I've just insulted her character. We're both having fun with this exchange—and I've just slow-pitched her a chance to make me eat my words.

"Uhh..." Finn cringes from across the table, catching our attention again. "That's a one. I rolled a one." He shakes his head disbelievingly. "The Prince of Thieves is... *not* starting this session off with a bang."

"Aw," Liv says, with a sympathetic pat on his shoulder. "Here, switch dice with me for next time. My d20's been lucky all day."

"The lock is giving me some trouble," Finn tells us with a sigh. "We'll need to take a different tack—"

"I use *Disintegrate Matter* on the lock," Emily says. She leans back in her chair and crosses her legs one over the other, holding my eyes with a satisfied smirk.

*Don't make the hot elf girl uncomfortable, don't make the hot elf girl uncomfortable, definitely do not flirt with the very hot elf.*

I take a very long swallow of my beer to prevent myself from saying something naughty.

"Er... *well,*" Liv says, startled. "That would do it." She rolls a die behind her screen and nods. "Julianna chants a single word and points her finger at the lock. An acid green ray of energy slams into it. The lock collapses into dust... along with a pretty large chunk of the door."

Emily's still holding my eyes. "*That's* why I'm here, baby," she purrs at me. "Any other questions?"

*Yes. None of them suitable for public consumption.*

"...huh," I mutter instead.

"Well, we *definitely* have to find some evidence now," Ginny sighs. "Otherwise we're going to have some difficulty explaining why half this diplomat's door is missing."

"Thankfully, that explanation would be Chief Diplomat Elsinore's job," Finn mutters to himself.

We spend the next hour or so investigating rooms, digging up all kinds of dirt and blackmail material in the process—some of which, my character quietly stashes away for a rainy day. The general atmosphere is pleasant; the banter is enjoyable. Before I know it, I'm three beers in, trying to prevent a thresher demon from murdering Ginny's borrowed royal character.

"Man, you know what we could *really* use right now?" Emily observes acidly. "Maybe a *paladin of Luin?*"

Liv grins at that. Her own player character, the paladin Elsinore, is obviously not appearing in this game, due to the fact that her player is *running* the game this time. "I'm afraid Elsinore is busy and cannot take your call right now," Liv says. "Leave a message after the beep, Julianna."

Emily purses her very red lips and finishes off the beer in her hand. "Okay, fine," she says. "Can you turn demons, Samson?"

"I can't," the cleric sighs. "I didn't take that ability."

"I *did* take that ability," I interject dimly. My brain is starting to slow down just a little bit from the alcohol. It's not enough to undo me, but I definitely feel a little bit silly for having forgotten such a basic aspect of my character. "That's not a bad idea. I'll turn back the demon."

"Ooh," Emily giggles. "The devil-worshipper is out-clericing you, Samson. You gonna let him do that?"

Samson snorts. "If you really feel that way, then maybe the *devil-worshipper* can take care of healing you from now on, Julianna."

"Maybe he can," Emily mutters under her breath. "Do clerics lay hands, or is that just paladins?"

I suck in a breath at that. *Don't hit on the hot elf girl,* I remind myself. It's not working. The hot elf girl is *flirting* now. That's like a green light, isn't it? I'm allowed to hit on her a *little* bit after that, right? "I am *excellent* at laying hands," I assure her. "I know a number of very lovely ladies who would be happy to act as a reference on my behalf."

Emily's very red lips part at that, and she lets out a soft noise. Her eyes are dilated, but I can't tell whether it's the alcohol or the flirting.

She uncrosses her legs. Crosses them again. Licks her lips.

Yeah, I'm pretty sure it's the flirting.

"Luke?" Liv interrupts my thoughts. "What's your roll?"

I blink and force my attention back to the game. "*Right,*" I manage. "One second." I toss my d20 hurriedly, calculating up the total. "That's a turn check of twenty-eight. I think."

"You think?" Liv sounds amused now.

"Your cleric of Berlisle could probably use a water or two to work off this alcohol," I admit. "Yes, definitely twenty-eight."

"You've made the roll with room to spare," Liv tells me. "Your unholy symbol flares with hellfire. The thresher demon cringes back, hissing at you... but it can't do much other than cower in the corner."

I nod slowly. "I think I'll ask it about its master. The rest of you might want to... step outside for a second. This could get unseemly."

"We're not going to let you torture that thing," Samson warns me.

"*That thing* is a demon with four bladed tails and a predilection for flaying its enemies alive," I tell him dryly. "You're not seriously going to tell me it deserves better?"

Samson hesitates uncertainly.

Finn considers this with a frown. "I don't think it deserves better," he says to me. "But *we* ought to be better than that."

"Says the Prince of Thieves?" I ask him wryly.

"Yes," Finn nods. "There was a time I'd have agreed with you, Devlin. But I've got to face Elsinore after this. I wouldn't be thrilled to tell her I let you torture some creature for information—not even a demon."

"Dame Elsinore strikes again," I sigh theatrically. "She's not even here, and she's still the bane of my existence." I wave a hand. "Fine. Kill it, then. We'll keep searching for proof."

The game hurtles onward. Soon enough, we do indeed have our proof of demon-dabbling. Ginny has the chance to dazzle me with the revelation that she's actually the queen herself. I'm really impressed with how much work Liv has put into the game as a whole.

I'm also desperately distracted by the fact that Emily has migrated to the hotel couch next to me. Somewhere in the middle of game, she peeled off those thigh-high boots and draped her bare legs across my lap.

"I guess... that's a wrap!" Liv says finally. She looks quite pleased with herself as she gathers up her dice. "I hope you guys had fun?"

"*Lots* of fun," I assure her. Liv beams at the compliment. Gamemasters are a bit light on the ground at the best of times, and I'm a habitual player. I consider it my solemn duty to shower my gamemasters with praise and keep them in the pool. "I hope Devlin wasn't too over-the-top for you," I add.

"Aw, no," Liv says with a smile. "It was fun trying to run a bunch of different alignments at the table. You guys all played great off each other." She pushes up to her feet, collecting up her bag—but Finn grabs it from her before she can protest, slinging it over his shoulder and pecking her on the lips. It's so adorable, it's almost disgusting.

"Great job," Finn mumbles. "I had a blast."

Emily leans back into the arm of the couch. "Oh, get a room, you two," she laughs. She's... probably not one to talk. The bare skin of her ankle has just brushed my hand.

"We *have* a room," Finn says humorously. "And I think we'll go use it. I'm actually exhausted, and I've got games to run first thing in the morning."

Emily grins lazily, but she doesn't respond again.

"You coming back to the room, Emily?" Jim asks, as he and Samson start packing up their own stuff.

Emily purses her lips consideringly. "I think I'll hang out a little longer," she says. I'm almost positive that's supposed to translate to *I've got another room in mind*. Ginny, god bless her, has pulled out her car keys.

"I think I'll head on home," Ginny says, with an arched eyebrow in my direction. "I'd like to sleep in my own bed."

If I have indeed got lawful good in me, it's rearing its ugly, do-gooder head right now. I close my eyes and suck in a breath. "You shouldn't drink and drive," I tell Ginny. "You can still use the couch in the suite if you want."

Ginny snorts. "I had a ginger ale, Luke. I'm fine. It's *your* hotel room, so go use it."

*You're a good woman, Ginny,* I think, as I open my eyes again. I try very hard to beam this thought telepathically into her mind. I might even succeed, based on the smirk she gives me.

The rest of the group filters out of the hotel lobby. I'm left with a bare-legged, redheaded elf in my lap. Her foot nudges my hand. I rub at it absently, and she leans her head back into the couch arm, letting out a soft moan of approval.

"God, that's good," she murmurs. "I love this costume, but the boots just *kill* me."

This. This is the best convention ever.

Emily smiles at me from underneath her long, dark eyelashes. "You mind if I hang out in your room for a bit?" she asks.

As though I'm going to say no to *that*.

"You can hang out in my room as long as you want," I reply hoarsely.

Her smile turns sultry. "Great. Just let me grab my boots."

Keep reading for a preview of Luke and Emily's book, *A Wicked Encounter.*

# AFTERWORD

I will always think of my father as a gamemaster. That's how he met my mother, in fact—she joined his 1st edition D&D game in university, and simply never left. What followed was a decades-long game that eventually came to include me and my sister as well. Eventually, when my father got too busy to be a gamemaster, my mother took over.

This was my introduction to gaming. You couldn't possibly ask for a more supportive environment. In the years to come, I'd run into a bunch of unpleasant gaming experiences elsewhere. But because I had played with good, caring roleplaying groups, I knew immediately when I was confronted with bad ones—and I rarely stuck around to get burned twice.

The main incident in this book is based on real-life experiences of mine, though it's actually somewhat toned down. I had a very uncomfortable Hero hit on me at a convention... when I was fourteen years old. Unfortunately, the gamemaster at the time did nothing. The flip-out that Hero had in this book was a separate experience of mine, maybe a year later; imagine, if you will, a forty year old man screaming profanities at a bunch of teens because someone dared to suggest he was hitting too hard with his boffer sword. Yeah… we pussified his game.

There's so much more, but I figure you get the idea already.

Many of these incidents happened five, ten, or nearly twenty years ago. If I hadn't had the strong gaming background that I did, I have to wonder whether any one of these things might have made me leave the hobby for good. But far worse than the incidents themselves was the silence surrounding them. Gamemasters looked down and tried to pretend that nothing was happening. LARP organizers never addressed the problem players. The few times someone ever stood up and said "that's not okay," it was generally a minority player who'd experienced that kind of awfulness themselves.

Not everyone had a great, wholesome game waiting for them at home when they needed to hide. Over the years, it's been very easy for me to see how women and minorities silently leave the gaming table because no one's looking out for them. At some point, I got so fed up with it all that I grabbed all my likeminded friends, started up a safer group, and basically hid out from the greater gaming community for a few years.

All of this is finally beginning to change.

Imagine my surprise when I sat down to an official 5th edition D&D game and got asked to give my pronouns and write down any subjects I didn't want the gamemaster to touch. I thought I was living in a different world. There are now explicit sidebars in official gaming books about the role of consent in gaming  There are Pathfinder modules with trans characters, D&D books with characters of color, and a real attempt to make everyone feel welcome at the table.

I can't speak to how effectively the broader gaming community is keeping minorities at the gaming table. But for the first time in a long while, I have hope that it wants to try.

In a fun sort of role reversal, I met my fantastic husband when I ran a game for him. Since then, we've run games together and even started a convention. And to this day, in spite of everything, I can't help but consider tabletop gaming to be one of the most romantic things in the world.

The future of gaming is bright. And as long as we all continue to look out for one another, it will continue to get brighter.

# ABOUT THE AUTHOR

**Ivy Collins** writes short, geeky romances with a hint of spice. She lives in Montreal, Quebec with her fantastic, prose-inspiring husband and her two cats. When not writing romance, she can be found running D&D or Pathfinder for her local group. She is a veteran gamemaster with more than twenty years of experience.

* * *

Want more short, geeky romances? Keep up with my releases when you sign up for my mailing list.

https://ivycollins.com
info@ivycollins.com

# ALSO BY IVY COLLINS

## Dating & Dragons

Dating & Dragons

A Wicked Encounter

The Paladin Wears Plaid (Forthcoming)

## Standalones

Date My Professor